Grandpa's Shed

Also by Robert A.V. Jacobs

Children's fiction, ten years and upwards:
Daisy Weal
Daisy Weal and the Monster
Daisy Weal and Sir Charles
Daisy Weal and the Last Crenian
Dauntless
The Adventures of Daisy Weal (Omnibus
edition, containing four of the books in the
series)
Cindy Lost and the Black Witch

Short Stories in the Daisy Weal series
(Available as ebooks):
Daisy Weal and the Grelflin
Daisy Weal and the Weenies
Daisy Weal and the Millions
Daisy Weal and the Face
Daisy Weal and the Secret
Daisy Weal and the Disaster
Daisy Weal and the Ghost
Daisy Weal and the Figment

Young Adult and Adult Fiction:
The Lost Starship
The Star Queen
Speaker (A collection of 31 short stories)

The Yellow Dragon
The Diamond Sword of Tor
Cardoney (Omnibus edition containing both
The Yellow Dragon and The Diamond Sword
of Tor)

Adult Science Fiction:
As a Consequence
Taldi'na

Adult Detective/Murder Mysteries:
Dexxman
The Disappearance of Natalie Firth
Time to Die
A Promise to Doreen
Almost Enough

Non-fiction:
Sudoku, Food for the Mind

Grandpa's Shed

A Novella by

Robert A.V. Jacobs

Grandpa's Shed
First Edition
Copyright 2016 Robert A.V. Jacobs

Pocket Edition
Published by
Robert A.V. Jacobs

Cover Background Image by http://www.freeimages.co.uk

This book is written in 'English' English, so there may be some differences in spelling to other international forms of English.

This book is a work of fiction and all characters are fictitious or are portrayed fictitiously. Any resemblance to persons living or dead is purely coincidental.

ISBN 13: 978-0-244-17237-4

Whether any of my scientific statements bear any relationship to actual fact is most unlikely.

Suitable for Children from ten to infinity

Acknowledgement

This story is dedicated to my wife Kim, who suggested it, though whether the actual story turned out as she intended is questionable.

Chapter One

My Grandpa says that it is not nice to talk to people without telling them your name first, so here goes: My name is Robert. Grownups, especially my mum, always call me Bobby, and I hate it. I don't mind Bob, but I like Robert the most.

Most of the kids call him Grumps, but I call him Grandpa Kenneth, because it is more respectful, and besides which he is much nicer to me than my dad. Grandpa Kenneth says that my dad is only being a dad, and as he is responsible for me, he can't be nice all the time, especially when I do something daft or bad. He says that *he* can be nice, because he can give me back when he gets fed up with me. I don't think he's had to do that yet though.

Grandpa Kenneth lives in our house, so that we can spoil him when he gets old, he said. That must be now, because I am pretty sure that he is really old already. I must admit that I do spoil him a little. I bring his paper and his slippers to him when he asks for them. I also bring him his pipe when he forgets where he left it. I moan at him about that and tell him it's not healthy to smoke, but he just says he's too old for it to matter anymore, and besides which he likes it. I don't agree with him, but as I don't want to upset him I keep my thoughts to myself.

Grandpa Kenneth has a shed in our garden. It's a bit of a wreck, as its made mostly of old bricks and has a really tatty wooden door. Even though the house belongs to mum and dad, they refuse to take responsibility for the shed. It has always looked old, and I can't remember it ever being any different.

I vaguely remember there not being a shed at all, but suddenly there it was looking just as it does now. I imagine that he put it together from any old bricks and stuff that was lying about. Then he started going on about replacing it with a new one, but money was always tight he said, so he never got around to it.

A couple of years ago he suddenly stopped complaining, and seemed to be making the most of it. It was very odd, and I couldn't understand why he had changed his mind, but he had, and he was my Grandpa, so I went along with it.

I have never been allowed anywhere near it, even when Grandpa was in the shed himself. It was the only thing that seemed to make him angry, so I stayed away. Grandpa himself doesn't go there much anymore, and he says it's because his joints are seizing up and he has trouble walking, but after some of his stories, and pretty far-fetched they are too, I am beginning to think that there might be other reasons,

"Come and sit down beside me," he said one day, when he was sitting in his chair by the fire, "I have strange and wonderfully weird stories to tell. You won't believe them, but I have to tell someone, so these stories are just between you and me Bob."

That's another thing; he calls me Bob most of the time, which makes me feel more like a friend than a grandson and pretty important I can tell you.

'The reason that I haven't replaced the shed," he continued, "is because I can't."

3

"Well I'm sure dad would be able to do most of the hard work," I said, "and I would be able to help as well."

"No, no," he said hastily, "not that sort of can't. I meant that I can't replace it because the creatures that I met there won't let me."

I just looked at him.

"The Tolltops are the nicest, and are my friends. They must be worrying now since they haven't seen me in a while." he continued, glaring at my obvious disbelief, "Don't dismiss things that you don't understand Robert."

It was pretty wet outside so I had nothing better to do, and besides which he had called me Robert, so I knew he was annoyed. I quickly apologised,

"Sorry Grandpa Kenneth." and then I asked, "Where did you meet them?"

"Have you not been listening?" he said, "In the shed. You meet everyone in my shed."

"Are they sort of like Fairies, or gnomes?" I asked, but I was thinking, *at least it's warm and dry in here, and this sounds as if it might be a good story.*

"No such thing as Fairies and Gnomes and such," he said, "They're just stories that grownups makeup for kids. No there are just Tolltops, Gridlins, and Tenpids. Oh, and I almost forgot there are Snerks as well, but it's

4

best not to talk about them."

At this point, I was pretty sure he was making up stories himself, but he is old, so I thought it best to let him think I believed him. Come on, I am almost ten years old, and nearly grown up. Did he think I was daft? *Play along Robert* I thought.

"I've never seen anyone or anything, apart from you, going into your shed," I said, smirking a little and thinking *get out of that!*

"Of course not." he said firmly, "Why would you? They have their own doors."

"So where are these doors then?" I asked, thinking I had him there.

"Inside the Shed Bob, where else would they be?"

"I think you are playing with me Grandpa," I said firmly, "I don't believe in Fairies, so why should I believe in Tolliflops?"

"Tolltops, Robert, Tolltops," he corrected, "and until you've been to Tolltopsy, I don't suppose you will."

"Tolltopsy?" I asked, puzzled.

"No, I'm tired now," he said, yawning and stretching his arms, "maybe if you don't patronise me, I'll tell you some more tomorrow."

As I have no idea how to patronise, not even knowing what the word means, I thought it was because I had been a bit off hand with him. I think he realised I didn't believe a word he said. But you never know with Grandpas. They know things, so of course I would have to look in the shed, now wouldn't I? As it was getting dark now, I decided that tonight would be as good a time as any.

It wasn't completely dark, so there was just enough light for me to see where I was going, I know I was in my own garden, but I still needed to see because if I wasn't careful I could easily fall over stuff that was lying about. It was usually me that did the lying around, but as I never collected the stuff up, I usually forgot where it was.

I felt quite safe knowing that I could always yell very loudly if I saw anything, and I'm pretty sure Dad would come running. I started to get a bit worried, because the sun was going down behind the shed, making it look all black with a sort of fiery outline. It looked pretty strange and feeling just a little scared, I stopped.

A hand dropped on to my shoulder and I almost jumped clean out of my skin. If I hadn't been just before I came out, I'm sure I would have wet myself, and then I would have been in trouble with mum. I turned around, ready to either run away very fast, or scream as loud as I could, but there was no need, it was only Grandpa Kenneth in his dressing gown. He was grinning, pleased with himself for scaring me.

"I was just about to get into bed when I remembered that you'll be needing this," he said, handing me the biggest and fanciest key that I have ever seen. It was bigger than my

hand, and looked as if I would need two hands to turn it, "but remember, whatever you do, do *not* listen to the *Snerks*."

I took the key from his hand, said "thanks grandpa," and he turned to walk slowly back to the house. It was really weird, because I wasn't afraid any more. Probably because Grandpas would never let you go somewhere if it was dangerous. Well they wouldn't, would they?

So I walked up to the shed door, and then turned around and walked back down the path. I had only thought that I wasn't scared before, when really I was only an inch from wetting my pants, even though it wasn't that long since I'd been. But I only went a few paces, realised that I was just being daft and went back to the door again. I did this at least six times before I could find the courage to put the key into the lock.

The lock was odd, because it was only about my waist height from the floor, which would make it pretty awkward for an adult, but just right for me. I had to wiggle the key a little, but eventually it went in. I needn't have worried about needing two hands to turn it, because as soon as it was fully in, the lock 'clacked' and the door opened.

I pulled the door toward me just enough to be able to get my head into the gap and look inside. As far as I could see, it was just an ordinary shed, with all sorts of shed stuff scattered about. There was a bench, a lawnmower, a garden roller and a wheelbarrow, and some garden tools hanging from racks on the wall. It didn't look at all strange. Disappointing really and I felt a bit let down. But there *were* lots of dark corners, and I couldn't see anything moving further inside, so I pulled the door all the way open ready to go in and check.

"Robert, its bed time," I head mum shout

from the house,

It doesn't pay to ignore any mother, especially mine, so I yelled, "Coming mum," and closed the door. I hadn't come across anything odd yet, but I still felt as if she had just saved my life.

As soon as I pulled the key out, I heard the lock clack as it locked itself, and I promised myself that I would really look tomorrow. Perhaps I might be braver in the daylight.

Fortunately Grandpa Kenneth hadn't told me what all of these creatures looked like, so at least I didn't have any scary dreams after I fell asleep. Well not too scary anyway. I did dream about the shed, but every time I saw it, it was a different shape. Once it even had wings, and another time, it was running around the garden on hundreds of little legs like a centipede. Even that didn't scare me, because at least it was running away from me and not towards me.

In the morning, Grandpa Kenneth asked me for the key back and said he would come down to the shed with me and show me around. When we got there, I could swear that it was not quite where it had been when I went on my own. I didn't say anything, because it had been dark, so I could be wrong. I did wonder why he was taking me now, when I had not been allowed to go there before. Maybe he thought I was grown up and responsible enough not to mess with his things in the shed anymore.

Grandpa Kenneth put the key in the lock, and my mouth dropped open. I was not staying here, so I ran back to the house as fast as I could. The lock was at waist height alright, but not my waist as it had been last night, but at Grandpa's.

I sat in my bedroom shaking like a leaf. I didn't realise I could be so afraid. It didn't make any sense, because I wasn't usually a scaredy-cat. My dad had taught me that most everything is natural, and if you think long enough then the answer will come to you. But a door lock that moves up and down a door on its own is not natural at all In fact in my little world it was downright impossible.

A timid knock on my door startled me, but I took a deep breath and called, "Come in."

It was Grandpa Kenneth. He looked a bit worried and sat down beside me on the bed.

"Whatever is the matter Bob? Did something frighten you?" he asked, "I can't imagine why you should be afraid. There is nothing in the shed to be afraid of, besides which I was there to look after you." Then his face took on a sort of really faraway look and he muttered under his breath, but I still heard it, *"Except maybe for the Snerks."*

"It was the lock Grandpa," I blurted, "it was as high as my waist last night, then as high as yours today."

He looked puzzled, "I can't see why that should scare you. Waist height is about the right height for a lock now isn't it? It would be a bit silly, if you had to crouch down to get to it, or find a box to stand on. No, it seems perfectly reasonable to me."

He smiled, patted my hand and then got up and left the room. When he had gone, I got the dictionary that mum had bought me for my last birthday, and looked up 'reasonable'.

Most of what it said I didn't understand, but I did manage to work out that it meant something that I would think was right. Well door locks that move are not right. And nothing that Grandpa Kenneth said could possibly change that. I was starting to think that he wasn't the nice Grandpa that I was used to, but someone who was beginning to look pretty weird

Chapter Two

The talk with Grandpa Kenneth had managed to do one thing, and that was to stop me being scared. I don't know why, because he hadn't changed anything, but he had made me curious. And in me, being curious was much bigger than being scared. Mum told me that it wasn't necessarily a good thing, and sometimes being scared could save your life. She also said that all kids think they are going to live forever, and it's the main thing that stops them from acting sensibly most of the time. But whatever... I am still curious and can't stop asking questions, which always ends up with Mum telling me that curiosity killed the cat.

Grandpa's Shed

Well I have no idea whose cat got killed, but it wasn't my Attica because he was still curled up on the sofa in the lounge. Perhaps it was one of those meta-whatsit stories they use to teach kids things, but whatever, even with all the questions, I'm still alive.

It still took a whole day for me to get up the courage, but eventually I snuck down to the shed. The key was in the door, so Grandpa Kenneth had to be inside, but I noticed a gap between the planks near the bottom, so I bent down for a look. At first it was hard to see anything, but by wriggling about, I got into a better position where I could see everything.

Grandpa Kenneth was in there alright, but it wasn't the Grandpa I knew. This one was definitely Grandpa, because I could see his face, but he looked much younger. Not much older than Dad I bet. That wasn't all. He was surrounded by at least six peop… er… things…

They were no more than the size of my arm, and were sort of like an upside down ice cream cone with two legs poking out from the bottom. The thought did cross my mind at this point that they wouldn't be able to see their own legs. They had the normal two arms, but they were long and spindly with some really nasty claws on the ends of the fingers. There was no head as such, just two eyes on stalks, a small bump with a couple of round holes for a nose just above a mouth that almost divided the body in half. I have never seen so many teeth. I couldn't see anything that looked like ears, but there were some holes that could have been ears I suppose. At first I didn't think it had any hair, but then I realised that what I had thought of as spikes, was really hair, and it surrounded his head just below the pointed top. I have never seen anything like it and I sat back away from the hole, panting.

I scrambled to my feet, hoping that they had not seen my eye looking at them through the crack, and hurried back down the garden path to the house. Before I got to my feet I had heard Grandpa Kenneth talking to them. Only a few words, but I remember them clear as day.

"**Laiceps si eh kniht ot smees MCP eht treboR no eye na peek ot evah ew.**" he was saying.

I shivered when I got into the house. My Grandpa had aliens in his shed. He could speak their language and it sounded as if they were after me. I thought of running down the road to my friend James. People called him Jimmie and he hated it. He didn't mind Jim, but he much preferred James. But no, he is my friend, and I couldn't put him in danger too. Besides which I don't think he is as brave as I am.

I was going to have to get to the bottom of this myself. No good telling Dad, he would just say it was me imagining things again and mum would just say, "Go and tell your Dad."

So it was up to me.

It was another two days before I felt brave enough, but eventually, making sure nobody saw me I tippie toed down the garden path. I couldn't believe my eyes. The shed door was open. The key was gone, so Grandpa must have thought he had locked it. I looked towards the house and as I couldn't see anyone looking, I slipped in through the open door.

It looked a lot like the last time that I had opened the door, just shed stuff and nothing else. Well there was a ball, and being a bit upset at not seeing anything, I kicked it against the back wall.

"Hey, that hurt. What's your game, kicking Tops about?" asked the ball. Climbing up onto two little legs he scrambled over the garden tools to stand glaring at me.

By this time, having already seen worse monsters, I was too annoyed to be scared, so planting my feet I stuck my hands on my hips and glared back. I was much bigger after all.

"Well if you didn't lie around all curled up and looking like a ball, I wouldn't have kicked you." I snapped.

"Can't a Top doze? I bet you wouldn't like to be kicked around while you were dozing." the ball said indignantly.

"I suppose you're one of those Snerk things that Grandpa Kenneth warned me about."

"Snerk? What gave you that idea? Of course I'm not a Snerk. Anyone with half some sense would know that. I'm a Tolltop, from Tolltopsy."

"Well Tolltop…" I started to say.

"I said I *was* a Tolltop, I didn't say my name was Tolltop. Are you all this stupid?" Interrupted the Tolltop, a bit snappish I thought. "My name is Binlod."

Still being a bit angry, I snapped back, "Binlod? Binlod? What sort of a name is that? What's wrong with Bill or Jim or Andrew or something?"

The Tolltop stared at me for what seemed like ages, but then he grinned. It really lit up his face and made him look a lot friendlier. I couldn't help it, I grinned back.

"We seem to have got off on the wrong foot," he said, "I'm not grumpy by nature, and I don't really blame you for kicking me. I suppose I must have looked a bit like one of your ball things. So will it be Ok if we start again?"

Just then, a bright thin line appeared in mid air, and started to slowly get wider.

"Quick," gasped Binlod, grabbing hold of my arm, "hide behind that roller thing."

I didn't need to be told twice. There were far too many odd things happening here, so I picked up Binlod and dumped us both behind the large garden roller. We crouched down, with just my eyes peering over the top and Binlod's around the end.

The bright thing had now reached a sort of small triangular door shape, and one of those upside down cone creatures came out. I sighed because I had seen Grandpa Kenneth with these, so they must be OK, and was just about to get up when Binlod squeezed my hand. He held me down behind the roller, and with his other hand he pulled my head round to look at him. He was telling me something silently by just moving his lips. It couldn't have been plainer. He was saying 'Snerk'.

I was shocked and almost shouted out in alarm, but instead I slapped my free hand over my mouth to stop any noises. Grandpa Kenneth had warned me about these, and then I had seen him talking all friendly like with at least six of them. It was all very odd.

The Snerk started to wander around the shed, opening drawers, various bottles and containers, and carefully checking what was inside them as if he was looking for something. We crossed our fingers, afraid that we would be discovered. We were lucky though, because he changed his mind as he was coming toward the roller, made a strange mark in the air with one hand and stepped through the doorway as it appeared. The door snapped shut and he was gone.

I wondered why he had left so suddenly, but then I spotted Attica who had sneaked in through the open door. He had spotted the Snerk and was growling way down in his throat, his fur was standing on end, and he was slinking along on his belly, getting ready to attack. Fortunately for it, the Snerk had seen him and disappeared before the cat could get to him. He might have big teeth and big claws on his fingers, but I bet the cat would have shown him who was boss.

Poor old Attica couldn't understand where the Snerk had gone, and kept pacing up and down and growling. I came out from behind the roller, and he immediately jumped up into my arms, his growl changing to a purr. He pushed his face into mine, and then licked me. I didn't usually like it because it was so rough, but he had saved us from the Snerk, so I thought I could forgive him just this once.

"This is Binlod," I told Attica firmly, "he is not for eating or attacking in any way. He is a Tolltop and a friend."

Attica looked at Binlod and then looked back at me, and I could swear he was saying, "Yeah right, and I'm a Snerk."

"No," I said, "he really is, and you have to be nice to him."

Attica jumped down and started to sniff around the Tolltop. Binlod started giggling, "That tickles," he said.

Oddly, after a few seconds Attica backed away from him, the fur on his neck coming up again, and then he stalked back to me and lay down next to my feet, but his eyes never left Binlod. I placed my hand on his head, and satisfied that he was safe, his eyes closed straight away, and he was asleep before I could count to one. I wish I could do that. It takes me ages to go to sleep even when I'm in my bed and supposed to be tired.

"Hey," said Bidlod, "would you like to visit Tolltopsy? I can make the door a bit bigger and I'm sure you could crawl through."

"I don't know," I replied, thoughtfully, "Mum and Dad would miss me if I was too long, and then they would get worried."

"Oh no," declared Binlod, "you wouldn't be missed at all. 'Cause you would be back almost as soon as you went, or even before you went if you wanted to."

Right then, the line appeared and another triangular door appeared almost exactly where the other one had a few minutes before and Binlod came through, and then there were two of them.

"Like this," he said, but I did notice that he didn't get very close to his other self.

"We can't get too close," said Binlod one, "because if we do we would sort of merge into one person. We wouldn't get killed or anything, but it's very, very, very painful. But not only that, it really messes with the time line."

Apart from the 'killed' part, I had no idea what he was talking about, but I thought it best not to ask. Besides which, my mouth was still open from seeing two of them.

"Well do you want to come?" both of them asked at the same time.

"Well ok then, but you have to promise to bring me back,"

"We promise," they chorused, but their broad smiles did seem to be more like a look of satisfaction.

Another but bigger triangular hole opened. I was glad that it was bigger than the one before, and I was pretty sure that I could squeeze through with a bit of luck,

"You go first," said Binlod, "and then I… we… can give you a push if you get stuck."

It was easier than I thought, and I soon wriggled through with them each pushing from a different side and making sure that their hands didn't touch. When I was safely through, I turned around to help them, but there was only one and he leapt through with no trouble.

"Where's the other you?" I asked.

"He's making another hole so that he can come back to just after I went, and then we'll be back to one again," he said by way of explanation, "and now to make sure it happens, I have to go back there, so that I can meet myself to show you what I meant."

Thinking about that made my head hurt, so I thought, *leave it alone and just don't look,* and closed my eyes. I opened them again just in time to see a hole open and Binlod come through.

"Now do you get it," he asked.

"Yes," my mouth said, but my mind was really screaming, "*No! No! No!*"

I was sure Grandpa Kenneth would understand though, and told myself to remember to ask him about it, if I could find him when I got back. But for the moment, I was in Tolltopsy, so I may as well enjoy it. I looked around. It was really weird, everything was triangular. Triangular trees, triangular houses, and triangular bushes. I even saw what looked like a triangular dog with really massive teeth, and strange triangular birds flying about. Oddly though there were no Tops that I could see.

"*Snerk! Snerk! Snerk!*" A really nasty snigger sounded from behind me, and I froze.

Very slowly I turned towards the sound, and almost died on the spot. The Tolltop was gone and in its place, and showing a great many nasty, very sharp looking teeth, was something else. I had been fooled. Desperately I looked around, but there was nowhere to run to. I closed my lips against the scream that was rising… I couldn't believe it… I had been kidnapped by a *Snerk*.

Chapter Three

In the next few seconds, weird thoughts went through my head, as me and the Snerk stood face to face. He looked full of confidence and I was scared witless. Judging by his odd behaviour earlier, *Attica had known something was not right*, I thought, *I should take more notice of that cat. No one told me that these creatures could copy other things. What do they want with me? Are they going to eat me? Where is Grandpa? How will anyone know where I've gone?*

Suddenly a round door opened next to me and what looked like a real Tolltop leaned through. I couldn't tell whether it was a boy or girl, but for some reason I thought 'he'.

"Quick," he said, waving his hand at me, "come through here. It's your only hope."

Somehow it was the change in door shape that gave me the confidence, and smiling at the Tolltop I said, "Just one little second if you please."

I had always been good at football at school, and the Snerk may have a lot of teeth, but he was only small, so as he came forward to stop me, I turned and aiming for goal delivered the best kick that I could. It connected perfectly and he shot up into the air tumbling over and over as he went, until he was stopped by a tree. His pointed top, hit the tree square on, and went in almost up to his eyes. The last thing I saw of him, as I slithered through the Tolltop's door, was his arms and legs waving about as he was firmly stuck in the tree.

"My name is Robert, but who are you and where am I now?" I asked, pretty relieved to have escaped from the Snerk I can tell you.

"My name is *Almost* Frettle, I am a Tolltop... we call us 'Tops' for short... and you are now in Tolltopsy" said the round ball who had just rescued me. Then he giggled "I must say that what you did to that Snerk was really impressive. I've never seen one stuck in a tree before."

"*Almost* Frettle?" I asked in surprise, though the compliment did make me blush a bit.

"Of course," he said indignantly, and then pointed at other larger Tolltops scurrying and rolling about, "see how much bigger they are than me. How can I be a *Complete* Frettle, if I still have growing to do?"

Well no one can argue with that, so I didn't, but instead gazed around. Everything was ball shaped. Round houses, round trees, round cars, and even what looked like a round dog. If nothing else, this together with the round door convinced me that I was really in Tolltopsy. It even felt nicer here, with so many Tolltops, all looking friendly, zooming in every direction. Somehow the other place had seemed a bit menacing. The round dog got closer, and I realised it wasn't really round, but more like a long round log, with a lot more than four legs,

"What's that?" I asked, pointing at it.

"Oh, that's only a Tenpid, he must be visiting sometop here. Gridlins come sometimes as well, but not as often as the Tenpids. We all can make doors, and come and go as we please. Well as long as the place has a PCM."

"What about Snerks?" I asked. I had no idea what a PCM was, and didn't want to look ignorant, so I thought I would leave explanations for later. I'm sure I'd find out what it was eventually.

"Oh my, you have to be joking! We would never allow any of those here. The PCM puts Snerk traps in any doors that open here."

"Come this way," he continued, and pulling in his arms and legs, he started to roll away.

He was really fast. "Where are we going?" I asked as I jogged along beside him, but I was really thinking, *how much odder can things really get around here.*

He stopped rolling, and I skidded to a halt as well,

"Sorry," he said, "but I have to keep my mouth shut when I'm rolling. You get all sorts in it if you don't. What did you say?"

"Where are we going?" I repeated,

"Oh I'm taking you home to see my mum." he explained. "We don't get many humans here, in fact, only you and Kenneth so far. He taught her how to make tea, and he said she was pretty good at it, so you can have some before you go back, if you want. We have lots, because he brought a whole load of teabags when he came last time."

I thought it best to keep any more questions to myself until we arrived at his mum's, so I closed my mouth and fell in beside him as he started to roll again. He could move really fast, and it was hard to keep up, so by the time he stopped outside of a house, I was pretty much gasping, but through my panting I promised myself that I would make sure his mum always had enough tea bags. I mean *Almost* Frettle had saved me from Snerkland so it was a small enough thank you.

"Here we are," he said, as he stopped at the gate of one of the large balls, in a row of seven or eight.

For a sort of round ball shaped house, it was quite nice, with nicely curved windows around the middle, and a round curved door in the front. The door was a bit small though, and I knew I would have to crawl to get through. I just hoped that my backside was not really as big as James kept saying it was.

I was lucky and was just able to squeeze through with a bit of help. *Almost* Frettle went through first and then grabbed my arms to pull me through. At first I didn't move, but then suddenly 'pop' and I was in. I just hoped there wasn't any cakes, or I just might not make it back out again.

As we entered, a slightly larger ball waddled out of another room and stopped dead as soon as it saw me,

"This is my mum," said *Almost* Frettle, "her name is *Virtually* Wendum. Mum this is a human and his name is Robert,"

"Pleased to meet you Mrs... er... um *Virtually* Wendum," I said, holding out my hand, which she took and then turned this way and that, gazing at it critically.

"It's just a hand." I said helpfully, "When we meet new people we shake each other's hand. My dad always says that it's a polite thing to do"

She grabbed my hand and started to vigorously shake it up and down, almost taking my arm off.

"Only a couple of shakes, and gently," I added hastily, trying to get my hand back.

Having had the '*Almost*' part of Frettle's name explained, I presumed that the '*Virtually*' part of his mum's name meant just that... That she still had a little way to go before she was considered to be all grown up,

"Would you like some cake?" she asked, eventually dropping my hand, and giving voice to my worst fears. Why I had thought of cake when I arrived, for the life of me I had no idea, particularly since I much preferred a pizza.

"That would be nice, thank you," I lied, suspecting that it might just be rude to refuse. Perhaps they had a larger door.

I did notice that there were no seats at all in the room, but then I realised that the shape of the Tolltops made it impossible for them to sit anywhere other than the floor. There were several thick mats, with roundish dents in the middle, so I guessed that was where they sat.

"Sit down," said *Almost* Frettle, folding up his legs and settling onto one of the mats, "and make yourself to home. Mum will bring the cake."

I settled myself down onto one of the spare ones, and found that it actually was quite comfortable. As I always watched the Tele while lying on the floor when I was at home, I didn't find it odd at all.

Virtually Wendum hurried out of the room, and returned in a surprisingly short time carrying a truly massive ball shaped cake, which she deposited on a low table that sat in the centre of the room. Retrieving a knife that had been tucked into her waist, she proceeded to cut some giant slabs from the cake, which she deposited on a plate.

"Help yourself." she said, pointing to the plate.

The cake looked amazing with piles of cream, icing, and pieces of fruit all over it. I was doomed. True I wasn't that keen on cake, but fruit, cream, and icing were my downfall. I would never get out of here if I ate that much,

"Could I have a smaller piece?" I asked, bravely I thought, because all I really wanted to do was to stick my face into the whole thing.

She gave an odd look, but then sharply cut one of the pieces into two, but *Almost* Frettle had no such hang-ups and was stuffing the largest slice into his mouth as fast as he could. I picked up the smaller of the two pieces and took a small bite. It was delicious and I was soon copying *Almost* Frettle and jamming the whole piece into my mouth. The second piece soon followed, and *Virtually* Wendum's face lit up and she pushed a larger uncut slice toward me.

I wouldn't have thought it possible, but the three of us polished off that massive cake in no time at all.

"I've got another one," said his mother.

"I don't think so mum. You can see what an enormous rear end he has," said *Almost* Frettle, quite rudely I thought, "Any more cake and we'll have to keep him. He'll never get through the door."

She was nice too,

"True, I see what you mean," she said, "but how is he going to fly without it?

I thought I had misheard her so I ignored her, thinking that it was time for me to change the subject before they could find something else nasty to say. They could talk. All they were was big round fat balls.

"Before I was kidnapped by that Snerk," I said, "I had gone into Grandpa Kenneth's shed looking for him. Have you seen him at all? He told me he visits Tolltopsy."

"No we haven't seen him for quite a while," said *Virtually* Wendum, "he used to like to come quite a lot, and we always made sure we opened a door for him at least once a day, but he hasn't used them for quite a while and we are now getting a bit worried,"

"Well that answers my next question. I could never understand how he managed to get here at all," I said, "I had trouble squeezing through the door and he's much bigger than me."

"You gotta understand how this works," said Almost Frettle, "Two or three of us working together can open a door big enough for your grandpa. It's still a bit of a squeeze, but he can just about make it. The doors are opened by our connection to the Principle Conundrum Manipulator, which we call the PCM. There is one in every reality and they are all linked. It allows us to go backwards and forwards whenever we want, if we connect with it telepathically." He paused for breath, "You remember the Tenpid that you saw, well he came for a visit from his own reality. But there is a small problem, legend has it that they all have to exist, or none of them work. Your grandpa found yours, but he should never have been able to open a door because your race is not telepathic. But he was testing it to see what it was and was applying elastrickery changes to it, and the door opened. It was too small for him to get through, but he did stick his head in."

"I think you might mean electricity charges," I suggested.

"Whatever," he said, "but it doesn't matter because we don't have anything like that here."

"But if the PCM already existed," I asked, relieved to have finally found out what it was, "why didn't you visit us before?"

"Let me tell you the rest," he continued, "Legend always said that there was a fifth key, that only one person would be able to use. It's said to be the key to the whole thing. No-one ever really believed it, but some of us kept looking anyway. We only went to places that we knew existed, so we didn't know about you, until your grandpa's head suddenly appeared. Frightened the life out of us, until we realised he was not a monster. But as soon as we knew of your reality, then so did all the other places.

The Snerks saw it as an opportunity to invade. Let me tell you, you wouldn't believe the number of times they've tried it on us. But we are prepared and they stand no chance. But you don't know about them or how to fight them, and when you do find out it will be too late."

He paused to make sure that I understood what he was saying, and to take a breath as it had all come out in one go.

"They may be small, but there are about a hundred times as many of them as there are of you. Your Grandpa said he would destroy your PCM and stop them for all time. None of us were happy about that, because having found it we now believed the legends. So we told him that he couldn't, because that would affect all of us. Instead we appointed him guardian of the PCM, even though whatever elastrickery he tried, he couldn't get it to work again. The Snerks were livid because we didn't ask them, and vowed to take possession of your PCM at all costs."

He paused again and his mum disappeared into what I presume was the kitchen, to return moments later with a round tray of glasses that contained what looked very much like tea with little wisps of steam rising. The glasses were like two thirds of a ball with the top sliced off and supported by three tiny legs. He grabbed one, took a huge swig and then continued,

"They got hold of it, but found that it wouldn't come with them when they opened a door. It just stayed behind when they left. If it hadn't been serious, it would have been really funny watching them try. Your grandpa grabbed it then, and tried to destroy it, but nothing worked, so he hid it. If the Snerks can't find it, then it's only possible to open one small door at a time, or with two or more Snerks working together a slightly larger one. It has been said that the doors have flexible edges, and can be stretched, but no-one has ever tried it. Instead they are relying on the fact that if two PCMs touch... like one from each side... then a huge door opens and they can pour through. Thankfully, they only found that out after your Grandpa had hidden it."

"So you know for a fact that it can't be destroyed?" I asked.

"Maybe it can, but we don't know for sure, and we certainly don't know how."

It had started to get dim in the room as the afternoon wore on, and *Virtually* Wendum walked to the wall and pressed a small recessed ball and some lights came on.

"I thought you said you didn't have electricity," I said pointing to the lights.

Grandpa's Shed

"Oh, was *that* what he was talking about?" said *Almost* Frettle.

Chapter Four

If I were to tell the truth, I really did not want to find out what they called it. I had enough trouble with electricity, so I decided to just let that one lie. The important thing was to find Grandpa and then get rid of the PCM thingy. There had to be a way, like maybe dropping it into a volcano or something.

"I've got to get back home," I said, "I need to find Grandpa, and then find a way to stop those Snerks for good."

Apparently it was not a good thing to open doors in the house, so *Almost* Frettle told his mum that he would take me outside and do it. You would not believe the trouble I had getting through the house door. It was definitely the cake that had done it. I struggled, he pulled, his mother pushed, but we seemed to be getting nowhere. I had visions of being stuck halfway through the door for weeks until I starved enough, but then a bigger Tolltop turned up,

"Oh, for goodness sakes," he said, and made a peculiar motion in the air with his hand, and the door suddenly doubled in size and I fell through.

"Hello Dad," said *Almost* Frettle, "this is Robert, and I'm about to send him home."

"Hello Robert," he said holding out his hand, which I shook. I wondered how he knew to do it, and then I remembered that they were telepathic, "pleased to meet you. I am *Complete* Lodtron, but just called Lodtron normally."

Being called '*Complete*' I assumed was because he was a full sized Tolltop. Really odd way of naming people I thought. But then of course being sort of big round balls they aren't really people. I don't know though, perhaps they are. They are nice, talk to me and have houses to live in. Wouldn't you think that would make them into people?

"Pleased to meet you too sir," I said, feeling that from me being a kid, the 'sir' would be more polite than 'Lodtron', "sorry I can't stay longer, but I have to get back home."

"That's fine son," he replied, "but let me do it, and give my regards to your Grandpa."

He waved his hand in that peculiar motion again, though I did see that it was slightly different than the last time, and a door grew in front of me. I could see the inside of Grandpa's shed through it, so I said "Will do sir," and jumped through. The door snapped shut as soon as I was inside the shed.

As I stood in the dim shed which was lit only by a solitary ray of sunlight coming through the single very dirty window, a sudden thought came to me. Did that thought make me cleverer than the Snerks I wondered? But could I be right, or could it just be wishful thinking? I couldn't be sure, but if I was right, then Grandpa was a genius.

Attica was perched on the garden roller, watching me, but then he asked, "Well are you going to tell us about this amazing thought or not?"

I did a double take, but his face was just a normal cat face, so I thought I was just hearing things, but I still asked, "Did you say something Attica?"

"No," he said, "I'm just a cat, and if you tell anyone that I did, I shall just deny it."

I sat on the floor in shock. My cat was talking to me. Before I had been kidnapped he had never had a word to say, but now he was talking. Had these other places affected me in some weird way? Maybe they had, how could I know for sure? But then I had another thought, and carefully imagined a door opening in mid-air. It was a good thing that I was on the floor, because otherwise I would have fainted, as right before my eyes the air went all misty and a door appeared.

"Close," I almost yelled in panic, and it slowly closed to a spot and then disappeared. I'm just a kid, but if the Tolltop's legend was right then I would be the only person on earth able to operate the PCM. *Why me*? I asked myself?

"*Because you are the one, whether you like it or not,*" came a quiet thought into my mind.

I almost wet myself at that, but instead pretended that I hadn't heard anything, and for the next ten minutes experimented with opening and closing doors, until I was satisfied that I could do it quickly if I needed to.

"Come on then Attica," I said, "let's go and see if Mum has seen Grandpa."

"If I must," he said, stretching and then jumping down from the roller.

The shed door was still open as it had been when I left, so I was unable to check out

39

my previous thought, but instead hurried toward the house with Attica following.

Mum was panic stricken, and told me, in-between tears, that she had not seen Grandpa for two days and had called the police. He had never disappeared before she said, so something must be wrong. Dad had stayed away from work to be with her, but wasn't a lot of use, as he kept suggesting all the horrible things that might have happened. I knew that I had been away for a couple of hours, but being so worried for grandpa they hadn't noticed, so at least I wouldn't have to face loads of questions. Then it occurred to me that *Almost* Frettle had said that I could come back almost before I went if I wanted to, so maybe I hadn't been gone long at all.

I knew the Snerks had something to do with this, but I am ten and not stupid. There was no point in me saying anything, because they wouldn't believe me anyway. So I kept quiet and instead said I would keep an eye out for the police.

The police when they arrived were not a lot of help. They just said he was over twenty one, a big boy, and he could wander off if he wanted. When mum said he wouldn't do that, they said maybe he just went senile and doesn't know where he is.

"That's what I'm worried about," Mum almost shouted tearfully.

"Ok then, we'll keep an eye open," they said, "but we don't have the manpower to actively look for him."

"Well if anything happens to him," growled dad, "watch out for the flack."

I knew what flack was, having been told stories by grandpa about his service life, and I hoped the police were just as informed. My dad can be a monster when annoyed.

"So it's down to just you and me then," said Attica, which was when I realised that only I could hear him. I didn't want everyone to think I talked to myself, so I just winked at him instead.

There was nothing I could do in the house, so I said I would go and search the shed and see if there was anything that might suggest where he had gone. Dad said he would go out in the car and see if he could spot him, and suggested that mum stay just in case he came home. They both had phones, so they could keep in touch.

When me and Attica got to the shed, I remembered being puzzled about the open door, so I examined it and realised that even though open, it was locked, which meant that the key had been taken out and the door deliberately left that way.

Not far from the shed was a patch of overgrown grass and weeds, and on a sudden whim I went over to it and started to search.

"Leave that to me," said Attica, "I can move through that stuff easier than you."

"Thanks," I said, "I'll check the shed over,"

Really there wasn't much to check, so luckily it was only a couple of minutes before Attica came ambling through the door with the key in his mouth,

"Look what I've found," he said, dropping it onto the floor by my feet.

I picked it up and knew instantly that I had been right. It was the PCM. What a brilliant hiding place. In plain sight, a door key for a shed, who would suspect that? Grandpa must have seen something he didn't like when he opened the door, and instead of leaving the key in place, he had taken it out and thrown it into the weeds as a warning to me.

So it had to be the Snerks. The Snerks had him. So it was up to me and Attica to invade the place and rescue him. We needed weapons. Well I needed weapons, because Attica had some pretty awesome teeth and claws. But what was there for me to use?

"Your Grandpa has a very nice sword,

which he keeps in that long box under the bench," said Attica, "not sure whether it would cut much, but it does have a nice sharp point."

I pulled the box out and opened it and sure enough a nice officer's army sword was inside. I knew what it was, because Grandpa had shown me all of the photos that he had taken as an army officer, and he had been wearing it in some of them.

"Perfect," I said, giving it a nice swing and almost taking Attica's head off. I had played loads of computer games where swords were used, so I knew all the moves. Putting them into practice for real though, might be a bit different, but that I would only find out when I tried.

"Whoa boy." said Attica, ducking, "Be careful with that thing."

"Whoops sorry," I said, and laid the sword on the bench.

I tried the belt on, but it was too big, so I put it, together with the thing that the sword was in, (scabbard I remembered) back into the box. It would just be me, Attica, and the sword on this rescue mission.

Chapter Five

"Are you ready Attica," I asked, preparing to open the door into Snerkland, but as it happened, I didn't need to.

I knew it was going to happen almost as soon as it did. A door opened between me and the bench, but the trouble was that I had not opened it. It had Snerk written all over it, because the door was very wide at the bottom and then rose into a point about three feet higher, just like the Snerk doors I had seen before. Three Snerks came through, followed by Grandpa who just managed to squeeze through. But something was wrong. At first I couldn't put my finger on it, but then I realised that his skin was all shiny and tight looking, and I could swear that he had got larger as he came through.

I was about to say 'hi grandpa' anyway, when, "Give me that sword boy," he snarled starting forward. He never called me boy. Always Robert or Bob and he certainly never snarled.

I reacted without thinking as he came forward, and lifted the sword. He ran right on to it. I was horrified. What had I done? Had I killed Grandpa? But then seeing what happened next I realised that I hadn't. The sword went through his middle much easier than it should have done. With a horrible hissing, shrieking sound, and a big cloud of purple smoke, his whole body collapsed and I was left with a Grandpa shaped empty skin hanging on the end of my sword.

It hadn't been Grandpa after all. It was a Snerk copy. I didn't need any further invitation, and quickly shaking the skin off of the sword, I leapt at the first Snerk and skewered him. There was that hissing, shrieking sound again and I flicked the empty Snerk skin away. I got the second one as he was turning to flee, but unfortunately missed the third and he managed to jump through the gate.

"You Snerks let my Grandpa go," I

yelled after him, I was so angry, "Or I'll come and skewer the lot of you."

The gate closed.

Almost Frettle had been wrong. It hadn't taken any time at all to find out *how* to defeat Snerks, all it had taken was a ten year old and a sword.

I am not a violent kid by nature, and if it had not been for the fact that the first was an accident, and not a real person, I couldn't have done it. Even knowing that they were just skins full of purple smoke, I still felt sick at the thought. But I was angry, and if they didn't let Grandpa go then sick or not, I would go and get him.

I turned to look at the skins, and was surprised to see that they were melting into a puddle and then slowly seeping away through the floor boards. The smoke had already gone, so they were easy to dispose of after all. Apart from those teeth and claws they didn't seem to have any weapons. Maybe they had never needed weapons. Maybe they didn't even know what a weapon was. I think they had made a mistake with us. They thought that because everyone else was afraid of them then so would we be. But now they had seen a sword. Won't they be surprised when they come up against a few guns, and finally realise how aggressive we humans can be if we have to.

Perhaps seeing what a measly ten year old could do, they would be really stupid if they didn't realise that our grownups would be much more dangerous. You never know, it might even persuade them to release Grandpa. But if they didn't, they now knew that I would be coming for him.

I sat on the garden roller and waited. I had plenty of time. Somehow the PCM was giving me all the information that I needed, including the bit about coming back before I went. It was pouring into my head, and so was the knowledge that it was only me. Grandpa had done it once by accident using electricity, and I knew that he had never been able to do it again. So I waited. Grandpa Kenneth had told me to always give the other fellow a chance. If he took it then everything was fine, if not well that was when the fireworks started.

I had only been waiting for about five minutes, when I got the feeling that a door was about to open. It did, right in front of me, and a slightly the worse for wear Grandpa struggled through.

"They let me go," he said, "I've no idea why."

"They sent a copy of you," I explained, "and I'm afraid I skewered it and a couple of

Snerks with your old sword. One ran away. I knew they'd let you go. Did you know that they are just skin, purple smoke, and nothing else?"

"No I didn't. How weird. They were very apologetic though, and have even decided to send someone to the Tolltops and the others to apologise and offer to be friends. You must have scared them something fierce."

I got up, put my arms around him and hugged him, and then guided him to the roller to sit down and sat down next to him. I told him that he had been gone two days and that mum and dad had been worried and had called the police.

"They had you Grandpa," I added, "and I would have done anything to get you back."

"I'm proud of you Robert, you did well, but now I'll have to act forgetful for a few days," he said, "they're never going to believe the truth, so we can pretend that you found me in the street."

"We had better get you to the house then," I said, "Lean on me and for Pete's sake look *old*."

"Sure I'll lean on you… " he said, "I've no idea who you are… or for that matter who I am… but you seem a nice enough kid… Is your mum a good cook?"

"Shut up Grandpa,"

We giggled right up to the house door, arms around each other, and then took a few moments to get ourselves under control before opening it.

"Dad," Mum screamed, "you're ok. Where have you been?"

I stifled a giggle when Grandpa said,

"Is this your mum, son? She looks like a nice lady."

Mum took him by the arm and led him to an armchair, and then settled him down into it.

"What's the matter with him Robert?" she asked me.

"Oh, he's ok." I said, "He just doesn't know who we are or even who he is. I did persuade him that he belonged to us, so having nowhere else to go he agreed to come along."

"I'd better phone your dad, and then we should get a doctor out. I suppose I had better notify the police as well."

"You do that mum. I'll look after him."

She went into the kitchen for privacy, probably not wanting Grandpa to hear anything, and as soon as she had gone, I whispered to him, "Do you think you can convince the doctor?"

"I don't know," he whispered back, "we'll soon find out."

Grandpa was a good actor and the next few days were really fun. The police just said I told you so, and mum signed a statement and we never saw them again. The doctor was a middle aged surprisingly pretty lady who spent hours and hours with Grandpa. I think she was convinced after the first few minutes, but just kept coming back because she fancied him... yuk. Next they'll be kissing and I'll be really sick.

Under her care, his 'pretend' lost memory was slowly coming back. He was very cleverly making it look as though he was getting better, but she still kept coming. Mum was getting worried because of all the visits, and asked her why. She said it was ok. It was outside her surgery hours and he was an interesting case. Even though she seems to be a nice enough lady, I'm not sure she's grandma material.

The odd chance that me and grandpa got to talk properly in private, was taken up with me trying to get him to stop talking about Samantha Blake (the doctor) and him trying to get me to listen. It was Samantha this and Samantha that, and all I could think was, *Oh my God he has her first name already*. When she was there, I took to knocking on his door, just in case I accidently caught them, holding hands or something.

I told Mum what I thought, but all she did was to echo my first thought and say, "Don't worry, Bobby, she seems to be a nice enough lady."

So there was no help there, and dad wasn't any better. He had better be careful though, because mum had seen the way he kept looking at the Doctor, and her glare said everything. She might have thought the doctor was a nice lady, but not when dad looked at her she didn't. But I was completely outnumbered, Even James, who just said, "I think she's nice."

I might have to find another friend.

Attica was on my side though, "She knows nothing about cats," he said one day, "she keeps stroking my fur in the wrong direction, and that's really uncomfortable."

"We might have to bust her thermy thingy, as a lesson." I suggested.

"Thermometer," said Attica helpfully.

"Whatever… or maybe we could get the Snerks to kidnap her?" I said as an afterthought.

Chapter Six

So that was the plan. I had the PCM, because every time I gave it back to grandpa it reappeared in my pocket. At first he got very shirty and accused me of stealing it, but I showed him by giving it back. He took it grumpily and stuffed it into his pocket, and I smiled at him and took it out of mine. He was quite shocked I can tell you, but he was convinced after we had tried it a couple more times.

I had to tell him about me and Attica then. I really had no choice, so I told him that I could open the doors to the other places as well. At first he didn't believe me, until I showed him by getting Attica to do a load of different things, like stand on two legs, lie on his back, and lift his right paw, that sort of stuff. It's a good thing Attica cooperated, or I would have looked really stupid. Then I took him down to the shed and opened a door just to show him that I could.

"This is amazing," he said, "I've been to those places loads of times, but I've never been able to open a door to them, apart from once when I used an electric current. You must be special Robert, very special indeed."

I blushed a bit at that, and turned my head away. Ok so grandpa's always think their grandkids are special, but you don't go around embarrassing them by telling them that do you?

He told me to take care if I visited anywhere, but he was going back to the house to lie down because he felt tired. A likely story… it was coming up to Doctor Samantha's time to visit, was more like the truth. Grownups are really not safe to be let out on their own.

But if I was going to put my plan into operation, then I had to get her into the shed. When I really thought about it though, I couldn't do it. I'm not really a nasty kid, misbehave sometimes it's true, but not nasty, and besides which there was no way to know what the Snerks would do once they had her in

Snerkland.

I was a bit tied up with school for the next couple of days, but on Saturday, I realised that mum had been looking like thunder for some time, which is not usual for her, not usual at all. I waited until we were alone, and then I asked, "Why the angry face, Mum?"

"Because," she said, slamming the drawer shut that she had been looking into, "I caught your Grandpa *kissing* that woman."

"But you said she seems a nice enough lady,"

"As a friend, yes," she said through clenched teeth, "but *kissing*… That woman is *not* moving in here."

"It's all very odd," she added, "she's half his age and not bad looking. She could probably get any man she wanted. So what does she want with an old crock like your Grandpa?"

She was right. Grandpa is a nice enough bloke, but hardly worth the amount of attention that he seemed to be getting from the doctor. Alarm bells started to ring.

So I thought, what if I follow her? Maybe I'll find out what she's up to.

The first time didn't achieve much, because I lost her. I was following, taking advantage of all the cover I could see, just like the SAS I had seen in the movies, when she turned a corner and vanished.

Well not sort of 'poof' vanished, but when I rounded the corner she was gone. I looked around, but the only thing I could hear was a cat or a rabbit of something rustling through the bushes by the side of the road.

The same thing happened on the next four times that I followed and I was getting pretty desperate I can tell you. I was puzzled, so I told Attica about it.

"Do you hear the bushes rustling every time?" he asked.

"Yes," I said, wondering what he was getting at.

"That's your answer then," he said, "she's gotta be jumping into the bushes."

"Don't be daft, she's much too big, and it would be more of a crashing than a rustling."

"Perhaps she's a witch and changes into something else."

"I dunno why I ask you anything." I said, and stomped back to the house.

But what he said stayed with me, and maybe it was that that prompted me to get the old binoculars that Grandpa Kenneth had given me and focus them on his shed in the garden. I didn't have to wait for very long, when I saw one of the old planks of wood that make up the door open upwards. Strange that I hadn't noticed that when I peeked through the gap. A Snerk wriggled through the hole, and then walked around the shed and out of my sight. My mouth dropped open, and my eyes almost popped out of my head, as Doctor Samantha came into view a few seconds later.

Attica had been almost right. She wasn't a witch though, she was a Snerk, and that in my book was just as bad. But how was I going to tell Grandpa Kenneth? From what I had seen he was too far gone to listen, and besides which how could he admit that he had *kissed* a Snerk?

Yuk yuk, yuk yuk, yuk... how nasty is that?

I couldn't tell him, so what was I going to do? I couldn't even tell mum or dad, because they wouldn't believe me. Perhaps I could hide behind the shed, and skewer her as she appeared, and then present grandpa with her skin before it melted. But thinking about that, I knew it would be gone before I made it to the house. He had to see it for himself. Somehow I had to find an excuse to get him up here to use the binoculars.

I had to give the Snerks their due, the copy of grandpa had not been very good, but this one was perfect. Samantha-Snerk had fooled me, and I'd been pretty close. Her skin had looked real, not tight and shiny as it had been on Grandpa-Snerk, and nothing she had done had given her away. So they learn from their mistakes it seems, and much quicker than I expected.

They had promised grandpa that they would be good and try to make friends with the Tolltops, Gridlins, and Tenpids, but it was obvious that their word meant nothing. I would have to warn the others to be on their guard. These Snerks had something planned and whatever it was, it wasn't good.

Mum and dad insisted on a day out at a theme park on Sunday, thinking that it would be a nice treat for me. Wrong! I hate the places. I hate dodgems. I hate carrousels. I hate chucking balls at coconuts, and I really hate roller coasters. I've even told my parents that I hate the things, but all dad would say was 'don't be silly all kids love fairgrounds'. So for me it was a thoroughly miserable day, and I was relieved when we got back home.

Grandpa Kenneth was cuddling Samantha in the lounge when we got back, and I muttered 'Snerk' under my breath as I walked past. She obviously heard, because she glared at me, but I grinned and mouthed 'Snerk' before walking out to go to my bedroom.

I would probably be in trouble, like detention, lines or even 'write home to mum' kind of trouble, but I had to do it. I diverted from my usual route to school and climbed up the steps to the local Doctor's surgery, and wandered over to a lady who was sitting at the reception desk.

"And how can we help you today young man?" she asked, without taking her eyes off her computer screen.

"I need to make an appointment for my mum to see Dr Blake." I said, politely.

"Are you sure you've got the right surgery?" she asked, finally looking up at me. "We don't have any Doctors called Blake here."

"Well I'm sure that's what she said" I said creasing my brow into a puzzled frown, "Perhaps she's from one of the other surgeries."

"I don't think so, son," she replied, "I know all the doctors that practice around here, and I have never heard of a Dr. Blake."

"Perhaps I misheard," I said politely, "I'll go home and check with mum."

"Good idea," she said, dismissing me by

returning her attention to the computer screen.

So now it was definite. There was no Dr Blake, so she had to be some sort of an imposter. I was convinced that she was a Snerk, but it would have been silly not to check. So now all the evidence pointed to 'Snerk' and that was what I decided to work on.

I managed to avoid any serious questions when I got to school, by being really, really, sorry that I was late, and explaining that I had gone to the surgery to make an appointment for mum. After that the rest of the day soon passed, and I headed for home.

Mum was alone when I got in, and looked at me accusingly. I steeled myself for trouble.

"Did you manage to make that appointment for me?" she asked sweetly.

"Err no," I muttered, getting a bit red.

"I met your teacher at lunchtime, and she was surprised that I looked so well... Don't panic... I covered for you... I said it was for an annual check-up... so now you can tell me where you really went and perhaps convince me not to grass you up."

"I really did go to the Surgery," I explained, "and I did find out that there aren't any Doctors called Blake."

"Really," she said, obviously surprised.

"Now that *is* interesting."

I was half tempted to tell her the whole story, but she wouldn't have believed me so what was the point. Instead I said I was going out in the garden until teatime. I went straight to the shed and using the PCM unlocked the door. Carefully easing it open, I peered around the edge and was relieved to see that all was as it should be. On impulse, I dragged the door all the way open and went straight to Grandpa's sword box. It was empty. The sword was gone. What was I going to do now?

But then it came to me that anything with a sharp point should do the trick. So I started to search the shed. After shifting just about everything, I had to accept that anything that had a point was gone. But wait... the hard wood bed springs, that Dad had taken off an old bed, were still there, stacked in a corner. They were about a metre long, very narrow, and quite thin. Make a handle at one end and a point at the other and it would be perfect... my own homemade sword. It was a bit curved, but I'm sure that wouldn't be a problem.

I almost ran back to the house and up to my bedroom, and after rummaging about for five minutes I found the pocket knife that grandpa had bought me a few months ago. It would be a long job, because the wood of those bed springs was very, very hard, but I knew I could do it with a bit of effort.

Back out in the garden, I sat down on a garden seat near the shed, opened the knife and started to whittle. I only managed to slice off tiny pieces at a time, but at least I could cut it, so I settled down for what looked like a long job. I just hoped that I could concentrate long enough to get it done. Dad used to say that I had the attention span of a fly. I had no idea what he meant at the time, but I was beginning to understand more and more as each minute passed.

A few times, I got odd looks from mum and dad, mainly because I am never quiet I suppose, with mum even asking me on one occasion what I was doing.

"Just seeing if I can make a sword," I answered truthfully, and fortunately she left it at that.

Chapter Seven

It was hard, and lots of times I found my mind wandering, but I forced myself and carried on. It took several hours a day for almost a week, but eventually I had a passable sword in my hand. The week had been difficult, with the Samantha Snerk visiting grandpa more and more often. I had tried to talk to him when he was alone, but I only had to mention her name with a slight hint of criticism and he flew off the handle. So in the end I shut up and went back to whittling.

Out of curiosity, I had tried to open doors to the other places outside of the shed, but it didn't work. It opened them OK, but when I checked they had only opened inside the shed. At least I knew I could open them remotely, though what good that bit of knowledge would do me, I had no idea.

The amount of times that Samantha Snerk had started to visit was beginning to worry me. Whatever the Snerks had planned, the time for it was getting too close for comfort. As every day passed, I expected the whole world to fall on me. I got desperate, and turned to dad.

Well that was a mistake I can tell you. After becoming almost hysterical, I ended up without any pocket money for a month, grounded for a week, and right now banished to my bedroom. Sometimes, adults really do not listen. They always seem to think that everything has a logical answer, and no amount of argument will convince them otherwise.

So, you've got it. It was down to me. The safety of grandpa, and probably the whole world rested upon my ten year old shoulders. We were stuffed. I needed help, and the only place that I could be sure of getting that was in Tolltopsy.

But first I had to escape, and that was harder than you might think. Every time I would sneak to the door and open it, I came face to face with a growling Ogre in the form of dad and hastily withdrew to safety. There was no way that I was going to get out that way. No, it was going to have to be the window, and as I am not very good with heights, the thought brought me out in cold shivers.

Gritting my teeth against the terror rising, I quietly slid open the window. It was one of those sash type I think dad called it, and I slid the bottom pane upwards. The roof to the kitchen was just below me, and I slowly eased my leg over the sill. My leg was waving about in the air, with the roof a good metre or so below me, so I moved myself until I was sitting on the sill with my legs dangling, and then I slowly turned around.

Sliding backwards on my stomach, I clasped desperately at the window frame with a grip so tight, I almost made dents in it, and let myself slide out. You can guess what a relief it was when I felt that roof under my feet. I was so relieved that I let go of the sill. My feet slipped out from under me on the sloping roof, and I shot down it like a rocket.

It happened so fast that I didn't even have time to yell. Scrabble I did, but there was nothing to hang on to, and I whistled over the edge to land in a heap in a flower bed. It was a good job that I had built up some speed, or I would probably have killed myself on the concrete path. At that moment, I vowed never to do this again.

I quickly scrambled out of dad's prized and crushed Geraniums, thanking all my lucky stars that they hadn't been roses or anything else spiked, and glanced towards the kitchen window. Fortunately no one seemed to have noticed an airborne ten years old, so I hurriedly set off down the garden toward the shed.

I always carried the PCM with me now, for try as I might I couldn't leave it behind. Wherever I left it, it always reappeared in my pocket. I had even tried locking it in my bedside cabinet, but it made no difference. When I put my hand in my pocket there it was, and to add to that, I also found that I was feeling uncomfortable when it wasn't there anyway. So as soon as I reached the shed, I took it out of my pocket and pushed it into the keyhole. The shed door opened, but I left the PCM in the lock, because uncomfortable or not, it wouldn't come through the gateway with me. Forming the correct thoughts, I opened a door to Tolltopsy, and stepped through.

At the last second, just before the door snapped shut, I looked back. Dad was standing in the shed doorway. His mouth was open and his eyes wide. He made to rush forward, but at that instant the door snapped shut. My last glimpse of him was that complete look of shock as he saw me disappear. Just for once, I had surprised him. I'm sure you can imagine how good that felt.

I'm not sure how they know, but a few seconds after I arrived, *Almost* Frettle came rolling up the road. He came to a stop right in front of me, but he must have misjudged because he was upside down. For a second he looked up at me, then grinning he reversed until he was the right way up.

"Hello Robert," he said, unfolding his legs and standing up, "dad told me you were on the way, so I thought I would meet you in case you had forgotten where our house is."

"How did he know?" I asked.

"That's just the way it is," he said, looking a little puzzled, "how could they be '*Complete*' if they didn't know what was going on?"

This conversation was starting to go way over my head, so I thought it best not to look too deeply. So instead I said, "Right then let's go."

He turned, pulled in his arms and legs, and started rolling rapidly down the road. I found I had to break into a trot to keep up, so once again, I was quite breathless by the time we arrived.

"What's that?" I gasped, pointing.

If I thought Snerks, Tenpids and Tolltops were weird, the thing I was looking at changed my mind completely. It was roughly the same size as *Almost* Frettle, but that was where all resemblance ended. It looked like a round sieve on legs. I could see right through the mesh of its body. Its head looked much like the handle of a sieve, only shorter and broader. It smiled at me! Well that's what I presumed the expression on its face was. And it did have a face which looked pretty normal with two eyes, a nose, and a mouth. The question I had was what happened to anything it put in that mouth. I really couldn't see where it could possibly go.

"That's a Gridlin. What did you think it was?" replied *Almost* Frettle, as if he was talking to an idiot, which I suppose he was, when it came to anything outside of my own safe little world.

"I really need to talk to your dad," I said, tearing my gaze away from the Gridlin.

"You're in luck. It's his day off, so he's at home."

I was quite surprised when we walked up his garden path. His house had a new front door, and it was at least twice as big as the previous one.

Almost Frettle noticed my surprise, and

grinning all over his face explained.

"It was Dad's suggestion. He told the council that if we started to have a lot of visitors from your world, it would be impolite if we couldn't get you into our houses. Everyone has a new door now."

If would have been impolite of me to refuse the massive amounts of cake that *Virtually* Wendum thrust upon me, but as her cake was absolutely second to none, being impolite had nothing to do with it. The reason that I was here faded into the background as I stuffed it into my mouth as fast as I could scoff it.

From the delighted looks on everyone's faces, I began to realise that I had accidently stumbled upon the right thing to do. If you are offered cake, accept it or you are insulting everyone. Yep, if all the cakes are as good as the one I've just eaten, I am really not going to have a problem with that at all.

"You didn't just come here to eat *Virtually* Wendum's cake, delicious as it is, did you?" asked *Complete* Lodtron, though I have to admit that it sounded more like a statement than a question.

"No," I said, "I believe that the Snerks won't keep their word, and are planning something."

I went on to explain about Grandpa Kenneth and Samantha Snerk, and about the fact that every sharp object had been removed from Grandpa's shed. I also told them about the fact that doors could only be opened inside the shed,

"So it's pretty unlikely that you will have lots of visitors from our world," I finished.

Complete Lodtron got up from his place on the floor,

"I've got to get to the council and warn them about this, and make sure the Tenpids and the Gridlins are informed," he said.

Addressing *Virtually* Wendum he continued,

"Look after our young friend here, and make sure he gets plenty of cake."

When he had gone, I just had to ask. I probably shouldn't have, because when the answer came I just sat with my mouth open,

"Cake is very nice," I asked naively, "but why do you always eat so much of it?"

"That's a silly question young man," said *Virtually* Wendum, "how else do you expect to fly?"

What she had said the last time I had eaten her cake came back to my mind, but I still protested, "But I can't fly anyway."

She didn't say anything, but disappeared

into the kitchen, to emerge a few seconds later with another enormous cake,

"That's because you haven't had enough," she said.

With the prospect of being able to fly, shoving the feelings of nausea from so much cake completely out of sight, I dug in. Lots of people would say I was a gullible idiot, but everyone wishes they could fly, and if there was even half a chance then I was taking it.

After the second ginormous cake and I wasn't feeling sick, I really got into the spirit of the thing, and was eating it almost as fast as *Almost* Frettle.

You can imagine my surprise when the third cake came to an end, and I noticed that he was hovering about half a metre from the floor. He laughed and pointed at me. I looked down and discovered that I was sitting up in the air as well. It was a bit of a shock I can tell you. I had to ask myself, what was in those cakes? I ate loads of my mum's cakes, forced to mostly, and never found myself flying. There had to be some magic ingredient.

"I didn't know you could fly." I said, "I haven't seen anyone else doing it."

"That's because we love rolling. It's much more fun, and besides which in the air you have to watch out for the Kriddles," explained *Almost* Frettle.

"What's a Kriddle?" I asked him, "and why haven't I seen one before?"

"That's because you very rarely see them until they are eating you. You can't mistake them. They are very large have two heads full of about a zillion teeth and four wings... Oh they do have a long tail with a nasty hook on the end. So look sharp we have to be quick."

He didn't need to tell me twice. The description was bad enough, so with him leading the way, we zoomed out of the house. It was easy, and a bit like walking. You never really thought about it, you just did it. It was fantastic. A few loop the loops and a couple of rolls later, I just had to get home and show dad. That on top of my disappearing through a hole in the air might just about finish him off. Well I hoped not, but I bet it would be a bit of a shock to his system though.

Almost Frettle pointed downwards, and I could see a doorway starting to form. I waved goodbye to him and zoomed right through it, to land with a bump up against the roller, right next to where Dad was sitting.

"I suppose you had better tell me about these Snerk things again, don't you Robert?" he said calmly, reaching out a hand to help me up.

He was surprisingly calm under the

circumstances I thought, but I'll soon put an end to that when I show him I can fly. I took off. Well in my mind I took off, but nothing happened. I really concentrated, but I stayed firmly fixed to the ground. I was disappointed. I had built myself up with the thought of how impressed everyone would be, only to find that, cake or no cake, it didn't work here.

We sat in the shed for almost an hour as I recited to him all of the things that had happened to me, and explained about the Principle Conundrum Manipulator and what it did. I even showed it to him and demonstrated how to open a door, but no matter how hard he tried, it wouldn't work for him.

"The main thing then," he remarked, "is for us to deal with Samantha Snerk, and at the same time let your Grandpa down lightly."

When we eventually came out of the shed, I leaned down, pulled my makeshift sword out from under it, and then locked the door.

"What's that for?" asked Dad.

"It's my Snerk slayer," I explained, "I didn't tell you, but all a Snerk is, is a skin filled with purple smoke. Stick 'em, and you're left with just a skin, which dissolves away in a couple of seconds. I used Grandpa's sword, which he keeps in the shed, but it looks as if they've stolen that, so I made this."

"Not bad workmanship Bob, but if you had told me this yesterday you'd soon be spending time in a place for the criminally insane, if I didn't chain you up in the attic first. For now though, you can consider your grounding cancelled, and your pocket money reinstated... with a small rise as an apology."

"That's nice," I said, "but I don't suppose I'd have liked the first bit very much though."

"Probably not," he replied, "but you can tell me anything you like now. You could even tell me that the moon is made of green cheese and I would believe you."

"Isn't it?" I asked innocently, and ducked just in time to avoid a playful smack to the back of my head.

"Convincing your mum might be the problem though."

Chapter Eight

When we got her alone, it was easier to convince mum than we had thought. She didn't believe us at first, until we almost dragged her to the shed and showed her a door. Then she believed alright. Though from the look on her face I still don't think she believes that I can talk to Attica.

At least I had some support now, and I didn't have to do this on my own. I had the two most powerful people in the world on my side, how could I lose? And don't tell me they aren't. Just show me a kid that doesn't believe that his mum and dad are superman and wonder woman, and I'll show you an idiot.

None of us could think of a solution though, short of walking up to Samantha Snerk and sticking her with something sharp. But as we didn't know how Grandpa Kenneth would take that, we thought it best if we didn't. I promised myself though, that if he announced that she was going to be my Grandma, then I would stick her anyway.

Out of the whole thing, the bit that really puzzled me though, was the first time Grandpa took me to the shed and I was convinced that it wasn't in the same place that it had been the night before. Nobody could tell me that it was. I notice things, and what I had noticed, was that the path up to the door was at least seven or eight inches out of line.

"Dad, am I losing my marbles? Or is this shed not quite in its right place?" I asked, as we all came out of the door.

"Of course it is," he said as he walked away. But suddenly, he stopped and turned around, "seeing as I didn't believe you before, and you were right, perhaps I ought to really look." He moved to the left and then to the right, "Well blow me, but I do think you are right."

"I agree," said mum as she came back to stand beside him, "but it's too heavy to have been knocked out of line. So what could have caused it?"

Behind the shed, the sun had by now settled down towards the horizon and the shed's shadow stretched out in front of us. The fiery outline that I had seen once before was starting to form. On impulse, I pulled the PCM from my pocket, and said,

"Lift the shed up as high as me."

I can't repeat what my dad said, as the shed lifted from the ground to hover level with my head. I had never heard him use words like that, but they sounded really rude. Mum just stood there with her mouth open.

"I see you've finally found out one of the other things that the PCM can do," said a voice from behind us.

We whirled around and I forgot the shed, which dropped like a stone. Without thinking I stopped it just before it hit the ground, and gently lowered it the rest of the way. It was an old and pretty rickety shed and if I had let it fall all the way, it would probably have smashed to bits.

It was Grandpa Kenneth, and he had walked up unnoticed while we were gawping at the hovering shed.

"You *knew* it could do this?" asked Dad crossly.

"I did," he replied, "but I could never

manage it myself. It was a Tolltop that showed me, but even he couldn't get it more than a few inches up. It seems that Robert is the only one that the PCM works for properly."

"And you never told us," said Mum, and I could see from her expression that she was just as cross as Dad.

"Would you have believed me?" he asked.

"Probably not, but that's not the point," said mum, illogical as ever.

"You do know that Samantha is a Snerk," I blurted out, unable to keep it in any longer.

I know it could have been a hurtful thing to say, but I was cross at the thought that he didn't trust us enough to tell us the whole story. His face was really sad, but he surprised us all though when he replied without batting an eyelid, "Yes Robert, I knew that, but I was playing along to find out what they were planning."

"Yeh right," I said, "and I'm a rabbit."

"No," he replied, "your nose twitches like one, but your ears aren't long enough."

"Shut up Dad," interrupted Mum, "this is serious."

"OK," he said wiping his hand down over his face, turning his broad grin into a frown, "perhaps I didn't *know* know, but I certainly suspected that something wasn't right. Let's face it, I'm not the catch of the month, particularly for a woman that looks as good as that and is half my age. Maybe it didn't occur to me that she might be a Snerk, but I did know that something odd was going on."

His gaze moved over us several times as we waited for more, then he continued,

"But how did you know Robert? They seem to have really improved their appearance, because the skin doesn't look all stretchy like it used to. It didn't even feel odd when I touched… "

"Too much information," said Mum, interrupting again, "there are children present. But tell us Bobby, how *did* you know?"

I grimaced at the use of Bobby, but she was my mum, and I could forgive her almost anything.

"I thought she was up to something, so I followed her, but she kept disappearing. Then from my bedroom window, I saw a Snerk come out of the shed. I thought it was strange, but I kept watching as it went behind the shed. When Samantha came back around and the Snerk didn't, it seemed pretty certain, but to make sure I checked the Surgeries and there isn't a Doctor Blake."

"We've got to find out what they are up

to," said Dad, "from what Robert has told us, they're a pretty evil bunch. But how can we do that? We can't just go there. We'd stick out like a sore thumb."

A thought suddenly occurred to me. *Could it be done? I had to find out.* I still had the PCM in my hand, so: "Turn me into a Snerk," I said.

"No, Bobby," Mum yelled, but she was too late.

The pain was really bad as it washed over me, and then I was on the floor rolling about and yelling it hurt so much. It seemed to go on for ages and then as suddenly as it had started, it stopped. I felt really weird, and looked down at two skinny legs poking out of a triangular body. It had worked! The big question was would I be able to change back? Was the effect permanent or short term? I pushed that thought to the back of my mind. It was a question that could wait until later. Right now though, I was a Snerk, and I had things to find out. I had never seen a Snerk smile, and didn't know whether it was possible, but as I looked up at the three open mouthed grownups, I felt one forming inside.

"Are you OK Bobby," asked Mum kneeling down bedside me, her face showing how worried she was.

"Yes mum, I feel fine, but boy did that hurt."

"I'm not sure I want a Snerk for a son, so hurry up and do whatever it was you were going to do, and bring back my Bobby. But Snerk or no Snerk… you be careful."

"Are you sure you want to do this Robert?" asked Grandpa Kenneth, "It could be very dangerous if they find out."

"Thanks Dad," said Mum "go on, why don't you worry me some more?"

I was going to tell her that I would be fine, but I didn't know whether I would be. The Snerk clothes and body just didn't have anywhere to hide anything, so I couldn't even take my makeshift sword for protection. I had spent a week whittling the sword, and now it seemed that I wouldn't even get to use it. For a second I felt terrified, and annoyed. Here I was about to go into Snerkland, not knowing anything about the place, or even how Snerks act when they're together, so from the evidence I had so far it looked as if I was pretty much doomed.

It would be a dead giveaway if I took Attica, so I stroked his head, and told him that he couldn't come this time.

"I understand," he said, "but you want me, open a door and I'll come running."

All the grownups had heard was me telling Attica hat he couldn't come, and the meow of his reply. So they were none the wiser.

"I've got an idea," said Dad, "change me into a Snerk as well. At least you'd have some back up."

It seemed like a good plan to me, though mum's sharp look said she didn't agree,"Only if I can be one as well," she said.

"And me," added Grandpa.

"And don't forget the cat," purred Attica, trying to make me forget that I had already told him that he couldn't.

Well it certainly looked as if we had the makings of a pretty good invasion force here, so, "Dad first then," I said, trying to grin, but when I failed, I realised Snerks just had a permanently miserable face. I had a fairly good idea that it wouldn't work, and I wouldn't be able to change them, but of course I had to try.

I opened the hand that had been clenching the PCM ever since I had changed, and announced, "Change Dad into a Snerk,"

We waited, but as I had suspected, nothing happened.

"**Change Dad into a Snerk**," I announced again, but a little louder.

Still nothing happened, so instead I said, "Change Mum into a Snerk,"

Still nothing,

"It seems that it only works for the person who is actually holding the PCM," observed Grandpa, "perhaps we can take it in turns to hold it and change ourselves."

By now, I was convinced that the PCM would only work for me, but I handed it to Dad, who took a deep breath and then said, "Change me into a Snerk,"

I have to give them credit for trying, but no matter what they did, they stayed as they were. In the end it was mum who sighed and said, "It looks like it only works for you Bobby. But I still don't like you going alone. Couldn't you go and talk to that *Almost* Frettle… um… person that you told us about."

When I had talked to *Almost* Frettle, he had not seemed particularly scared of the Snerks, so it sounded like a good idea to me, but I couldn't risk being caught in one of their Snerk traps, so, "Change me into a Tolltop," I said.

As I had expected, it hit me again. The pain was worse than the last time, and my rolling body only came to a stop when Mum and Dad grabbed hold of me. After a couple of experimental twists they finally found the right way up, and settled me onto my legs.

"I wasn't all that keen on the Snerk," said

Mum, poking me in the middle and making me giggle, "but this is really cute."

"You'd better get on with this Robert," said Grandpa Kenneth, "Time's a wasting, and we don't know how long you'll stay like that."

"Ok," I said and went over to the shed door. As I was now only about the size of a football, and the door lock was at the waist height of my person form, I reached up toward the lock. I needn't have bothered though, because as I reached for it, it slid down the door and stopped at the right height for me to push in the PCM.

"You were right Robert," said Grandpa, "it does move."

I had discovered that as long as I was reasonably close to the key, it still worked, so I climbed up over the door sill and experimentally rolled into the shed. I came to a stop up against the garden roller but then had to roll back until I was the right way up, sticking my legs down to steady myself.

"Open a door to Tolltopsy," I said.

When I was in my normal person form, any doors I opened had been person shaped, but now as a Top, I was relieved to see that as the door started to form it was Top shaped. I shouted, "see you later," and dived through the hole. Hoping that I still had enough cake in my system, I experimentally hopped into the air, and was delighted as I zoomed upwards.

Chapter Nine

The door closed and within seconds I was well into the air and heading towards where I knew *Almost* Frettle's house to be. The whole thing had been so quick, that when I could see no one arriving where the door had appeared, I realised that it was possible that no one had noticed my arrival. Not to worry, I knew where his house was, so I could surprise him with my appearance.

I angled my flight toward the group of houses where I knew his to be, but was suddenly brought to a stop by a massive shadow over my head, and a huge hooked tail that wrapped around my middle. My immediate thought was,

"Kriddle," and I couldn't hold back the scream that ripped from my throat.

As I looked up, all I could see was teeth. Millions it seemed, all waiting to eat me. I struggled and screamed even louder. But it wasn't any good. I couldn't get out of the grip that the tail had on me, and I was being drawn toward the teeth. I was becoming frantic as one mouth opened and the tail brought me toward it. But suddenly the mouth snapped shut and instead I was brought to a stop in front of an eye.

"Ere...you aren't a Top," said the Kriddle, "you only look like one, but you don't smell right at all."

Well as no one had told me that Kriddles could talk, I was pretty much gobsmacked I can tell you, relieved that it didn't look as if I was going to be eaten its true, but still gobsmacked.

"Well what have you got to say for yourself?" demanded the Kriddle, shaking me up and down in front of its eye.

"M.m.m.y n.n.n.ame is.s.s R.r.r.obert," I eventually managed to get out, "I.i.i'm a.a.a h.u.u.man."

"Interesting," said the Kriddle, "you do understand that it doesn't mean that I won't eat you. But I am prepared to listen to reasons why

I shouldn't."

"I would be thoroughly unpleasant to eat," I said, trying hard to sound convincing as I became more confident.

"Why?" asked the Kriddle, "How do you know what I like?"

"OK then," I said, "you tell me. For instance what does a Top taste like?"

"They are all gooey inside and taste a bit like marshmallows," said the Kriddle, licking its lips at the thought.

I didn't stop to worry about how a Kriddle could know what marshmallows taste like, but hurriedly blurted out,

"Well I taste like blood and bone and flesh," I said, "nothing at all like marshmallows."

"Eek, Yuk, how revolting," said the Kriddle, "that's disgusting. How could anyone eat one of you?"

"Well usually no one does," I replied.

"That's stupid," declared the Kriddle, "what use are you, if no one eats you?"

"Not everyone is here just to be eaten. We have other uses as well."

"Yeh, what for instance?" he asked, "If you didn't want to be eaten, why did you come all dressed up as a Top? Maybe if I took just a little nibble...?"

87

I couldn't for the life of me think of a quick answer to his first question, so I ignored it,

"I would rather you didn't, and anyway I came looking for help against the Snerks," I said.

"Now you're talking. Maybe I won't eat you after all. Snerks are definitely something that we can help you with," said the Kriddle, "we don't get nearly enough of those. All full of purple stuff, makes us high as kites, but it is filling. You bring them to us, and we'll eat them for you."

"Can I go then?" I asked, hoping that he was truly convinced that I wouldn't be worth eating.

"Oh yes, sorry. I didn't think. Will you be ok if I just let go, or would you like me to put you down somewhere?"

"Put me down on the ground... anywhere will do," I said, not sure whether I had any flying left in me.

"We used to get a lot of Snerks," he said conversationally as we headed downwards, "but then the Tops set up those Snerk traps and the supply dried up. Gridlins have no substance to talk of, and Tenpids insides are all wiggly and not at all pleasant. So we have to eat more and more Tops just to get by."

"Thanks," I said as he deposited me on the ground, "My name is Robert, what's yours?"

"I'm called Kriddle Fifteen Seventy-Two, but you can call me Eighty-seven for short."

I tried, but for the life of me I could not see any connection between Fifteen Seventy-two and Eighty-seven, but then it struck me. If you add fifteen to seventy-two then you end up with eighty-seven... weird, but who was I to question how Kriddles named themselves.

As luck would have it, we had landed quite near to *Almost* Frettle's house, and I could see him peering abound the side, so I waved to the Kriddle as it took off and then headed toward the house.

"Who are you, and why didn't that Kriddle eat you?" he snapped as he jumped out and faced me.

"It's me... Robert," I said, "and the Kriddle realised that I wasn't a Top."

"Hey Robert how are you? You're looking good."

He came up to me and hugged me as if he hadn't seen me in years, then we went into his house. His Mum and Dad were both at home, and I wasted no time in telling them the whole story.

"Well that answers several questions," said *Complete* Lodtron, "such as why the number of Tops lost to Kriddles has increased so much, and why the Snerks have gone so quiet. We originally put it down to their recent agreement with us, but when I think about it, Robert's story makes more sense, so we need to find out what they are up to."

I tried to remember what Mum and Dad had said about drugs and how they affected people. I didn't really understand everything, but I did know enough to know that with a steady supply of Snerks the Kriddles wouldn't be able to resist them. They would become addicted and leave the Tops alone.

In a way it would be a shame, but there wouldn't be enough in the Snerks to keep the Kriddles fed, but being addicted they wouldn't care and would probably die out in fairly short order. I wasn't happy about it, but in the end it was really a clear choice between the Tolltops and the Kriddles.

Complete Lodtron said that he would convince the Council that they needed to instruct their PCM to disable the Snerk traps in the doors as a first step, and then gather up a few friends to go with me into Snerkland.

He hurried off to make his arrangements, leaving me and *Almost* Frettle with *Virtually*

Wendum, who wasted no time before placing some enormous cakes on the table. She kept smiling at me and rubbing my head, and then calling me *Almost* Robert as we tucked enthusiastically into them. I had the feeling that she wanted to adopt me. It would be nice, but I would miss my own Mum and Dad, so I kept talking about them. After a while, she got the message and smiling sadly said,

"I understand Robert. I would really like you to stay, but I promise I won't almostnap you. Your Mum is very lucky."

After a couple of hours, in which I consumed about ten kilogrammes of cake, I was feeling so light that I had trouble staying on the ground, so In the end I gave up trying and just enjoyed floating about. *Virtually* Wendum explained that we needed as much as we could get, if we wanted any chance of a successful invasion of Snerkland. Apparently Snerks could fly as well when they ate cake, but as it also made them sick, they only used it as a last resort.

When *Complete* Lodtron eventually came back, he was accompanied by at least twenty *Almosts*, and at my puzzled look told me that anyone larger than an *Almost* could not change into a Snerk, or anything else for that matter. I told him that I had changed into one, and I was much larger, but he just shrugged and said it didn't work for Tolltops. The only question I had left was whether an invasion force consisting of only kids was a good idea.

I had hoped that at least some *Completes* would be along to look after the rest of us, but when I asked whether it really would be a good idea to let just *Almosts* go, he said sadly,

"We lose a good fifty percent of our *Almosts* through one accident or another, not to mention those that are eaten by Kriddles. So they are used to danger. We don't force them, nor do we stop them. These are all volunteers, and they all know that it is our very existence that is at stake. And besides which there isn't any alternative is there?"

Knowing how most grownups felt about kids in my world, I thought his response was a bit strange, but then Grandpa Kenneth's words came back to me, "Everyone is different; don't judge them by your standards, but by their own."

I hadn't really understood much of what he said at the time, but I now as I looked around at the mass of young and enthusiastic faces, I knew what he meant. In their own society, everyone who could, *did*, and everyone who *couldn't*, turned to them.

"Your world is used to wars and

violence, much more so than ours, so this army is yours. You are in charge General Robert." *Complete* Lodtron finished in tones that couldn't be argued with.

I had been hoping that there would be someone to tell me what to do. I certainly hadn't expected that I would have to be the one doing the telling. I am only ten for God's sake. Hardly old enough to ride a two wheeled bike let alone lead an army. But it looked like that was exactly what I was about to do. I had to sound confident, even if I didn't feel it. Some sensible decisions were needed and fast.

"Ok Soldiers," I said as firmly as my trembling voice would allow, "We need weapons. Anything long and sharp will do, but it must be long enough so that you can stick them out of range of their arms and teeth. Remember we are not there just to attack everything we see. We are there to gather information, so only stick them in self-defence."

"Nicely put Robert," said *Complete* Lodtron.

I ignored him, but continued with just a little more confidence,

"As soon as we pass through the gate, we head off individually in every direction. Avoid Snerks where you can, and make up something plausible to explain the long sharp stick you are carrying. Find out as much as you can. We will meet back at the gate position one hour later. Don't be late. We can't jeopardise everything, and we *will* leave whether you are all there or not. Now go and find your weapons. Be back in thirty minutes."

As one, they all turned and rushed off in every direction, looking a lot more confident and certainly with more enthusiasm than I had. I watched until the last one had gone and then I turned to *Complete* Lodtron,

"There is something I have to do, before we go." I said, and headed for the door.

Once outside, I kept myself as close to the ground as I could, moved a little way away from the house, and looking upwards screamed at the top of my voice,

"**Eighty-Seven**."

I shouted several times, but when he didn't appear, I finally gave up and started floating back toward the house. I had only moved a couple of metres when the sky above me darkened and the characteristic screech of the Kriddle almost deafened me.

"What!" he said, a little abruptly I thought as he landed in front of me.

"If you hang around when the gates are opened, you might manage to snatch a Snerk or two. The Snerk traps have been disabled. But I am taking an army through. We have to look like Snerks, and you have to promise me that you won't eat any of us."

"About time I must say. OK, I promise, but I can't guarantee that any of my friends will honour that."

As that was the best that I could hope for, I said thank you politely and zoomed back to the house.

"*Almost* Frettle," I said, when I was safely back inside, "you never told me that Kriddles could speak."

"Why would I have to tell you? Of course they can speak. Why wouldn't they? Sometimes you are really strange," he said, and then turned around and ran out of the door.

It didn't sound like a subject that I wanted to pursue, so I just mumbled something at his disappearing back, and dug into more cake.

I soon learnt how reliable Tops were when as the clock ticked up to thirty minutes, they all seemed to reappear at once. Without being told, they formed up into a passable group of three lines, and stood silently waiting for me. Each one had a long sharpened stake, probably three times their own height, and what surprised me most was that the stakes were identical, even the one that *Almost* Frettle suddenly appeared with.

I floated out of the house and hovered just in front of them,

"I need to see that you've had enough cake," I said, "so all of you lift up from the ground."

With them all hovering, I said,

"You all know what you have to do, so as soon as *Complete* Lodtron opens the gate I want you through it, one at a time as fast as possible. He is going to instruct the gate to change each one of you into a Snerk as you pass through. I will be the last one through. Good luck guys."

The gate opened and I couldn't believe the speed that they went through. Nose to tail, they rocketed away from their lines completely in order. It took me by surprise, and I only just managed to catch up to the last one. As I passed through the gate, the pain was just as bad as the first time, and I hit the ground on the other side out of control and rolling end over end into some bushes. Well I think they were bushes. Each one was triangular shaped and covered in triangular leaves. I had to stifle a giggle as it came to me that the only thing that would be at home here would probably be a Toblerone*.

***Toblerone is a registered trade mark of the US Company Mondelēz International, Inc.**

Chapter Ten

I only had an hour, so I needed to make a move. It wouldn't do for the General of an army to be late. The army themselves hadn't hung about, and were nowhere to be seen, so I quickly got out of the bush and headed off in the direction that I happened to be facing. It was a really weird place. I saw something that looked surprisingly like a cat, apart from being triangular, scampering into a triangular house. A triangular bird flew past, under a sky filled with large triangular clouds. When the sun managed to make it through a gap, it was triangular as well.

I shook my head. I was not here to

sightsee. Ahead of me, I could see smoke coming out of several tall triangular chimneys, so I picked up speed and headed toward them. After a few seconds, I realised that I was hearing a noise, which sounded like metal on metal as if it was being hammered. It only took about five minutes before I spotted the large triangular gates of a building that could only be a factory.

There were Snerks, hundreds of them, all queuing up at the gates and being ushered in one at a time. Across the courtyard, I could see another gate with Snerks streaming back out through it. It took me a moment, but when I concentrated, I could see that the Snerks leaving were different to the Snerks that were waiting to enter.

Each one had Grandpa's sword, and the main part of their body was covered by armour. So that was where Grandpa's sword had gone, the Snerks had stolen it and were copying it. They seemed to be forming a huge army, and against the armour they appeared to be wearing, our sharpened stakes would be useless. It really did look as if they getting ready for an invasion, but the question was who did they intend to invade first?

My world would make short work of them if they tried to invade us, what with guns, tanks and nuclear weapons, and some armour piercing bullets would have no trouble with the armour. Samantha Snerk had been sniffing around Grandpa Kenneth long enough to realise that, so the target had to be one of the other realities.

I had seen enough. I would be able to get back to the meeting point well before the gate opened, so I took my time using whatever cover I could find. I was too confident I suppose, and was not really paying attention, so perhaps my not seeing the large piece of wood swinging toward me was understandable.

I woke up, back in my human form, hanging from some ropes stretched between two poles. All I could remember was this massive whack on the upper part of my Snerk body, which I suppose you could call my head, and then nothing. It was really, really painful, and I didn't need to be a genius to realise that I was in some deep trouble.

In front of me were hundreds of Snerks in armour, cheering and waving their swords. A few were a little less than careful, and several puffs of purple smoke wafted up from amongst them. None of them seemed to care, and it

Robert A.V. Jacobs

didn't have any effect on the celebrations at all.

As I looked to my left, and then to my right, I could see that I wasn't alone, and at least a half a dozen Tolltops were hanging beside me. By my count that was fourteen who had made it back home.

I was brought back out of my thoughts, by a single Snerk who stepped forward. He looked exactly like the rest, except that he had three lightning bolts painted on the front of his armour,

"Snerk, Snerk, Snerk," he sniggered, "I don't know what you came here for, but whatever it was you're too late. We shall be in Tolltopsy by noon tomorrow and there is nothing you can do to stop us."

He sniggered again, "Snerk, Snerk, Snerk. But you won't see it of course. We have to feed the army somehow, and I'm sure you'll do just fine when we roast you in the morning."

He didn't wait for an answer, but just turned and walked back into the crowd. The sniggers rose to a howl of laughter as me and my friends struggled to get out of the ropes. For the rest of the day, Snerks kept coming past, and throwing some pretty unspeakable stuff at us, so by nightfall we had begun to smell quite ripe.

The guys tied next to me were obviously

in as much discomfort as I was, perhaps more given their body shape, and had started to moan. I felt really bad. I had brought them here, and probably sealed their fate.

By midnight, I was beginning to despair of ever getting out of this mess. Some of the Tolltops moaning and whimpering was getting louder, and I knew that they were just as terrified as I was. No Snerks had come anywhere near us for the past few hours, and blood was starting to trickle down my arms where the ropes had cut into my wrists. Everyone dies eventually. It would just be a shame to go before I had done anything useful in the world. It wasn't the dying that upset me. It was the thought of being roasted. Then what Attica had said suddenly come into my mind. Perhaps the PCM would let him pick up my thoughts.

With that thought giving me a little confidence, I reached out with my mind and commanded the smallest door possible to open, then I sent out my thought to Attica. I knew that if he got it then he would be here as fast as he could, so now all I could do was wait.

"Well, you are in a fine mess now aren't you?" came the purry voice that I recognised as Attica's, "I've had a look at the stuff they've tied you with, and sorry but it's too tough for

101

my teeth."

"Perhaps you can find someone to help," I suggested, though as only I could talk to him, I couldn't imagine how that would work.

"I'll try," he replied, "though you do know that it might be difficult to make them understand."

A slight rustling behind me told me that he was leaving, so all I could now was to wait and hope. At least an hour passed, and I was beginning to face the fact that no help was ever likely to turn up, But then, "Pssst," said a voice behind me.

At first I thought I was hearing things, but no, there it was again,

"Pssst"

"I can't see you," I said, straining my head around as far as it would go.

"I'll come around," said the voice in a whisper.

I confess that I was speechless as she came into view. It was Samantha Snerk, and her eyes kept darting sideways. She was frightened I could tell, but she still stood her ground as she waited for me to speak. Eventually I managed a croaked,

"What are you doing here, and why are you still Samantha?"

"Well for the first part, Attica came and

told me, but for the rest it's a long story," she said, "but first we have to get you out of here. I wouldn't be able to face your grandpa ever again if anything happened to you."

She looked around, and eventually spotted a sword lying on the ground next to a small wet patch. Obviously one of the victims of the previous evening's celebrations, and no one had bothered cleaning up. She quickly went over and picked it up. Returning, she severed the ropes holding me with a couple of well-placed swings and as I fell, went on to release the Tolltops.

"Come on," she said, grabbing my hand and hauling me to my feet, "we can grab a Snerk when we get to the rendezvous, and make him open a gate for us."

"We don't need another Snerk. We have you," I said.

"Sorry," she said, pulling me along even faster, "but it doesn't work that way. I'll tell you the whole story when we get back… If we get back."

Something in her voice gave me the trust I needed,

"It seems that each of the five PCM's operate slightly differently." I said breathlessly, "At home ours will only work for me. Here it works for anyone who has the ability to project thoughts to it. Somehow I know that only Tolltop adult males can influence theirs and Gridlin females theirs. With Tenpids it's the children."

"Why are you telling me this now?" she asked.

"Simple really, we don't need a Snerk... I can open a gate myself."

"We're here," she said coming to a stop, and only avoiding being bowled over by the rolling Tolltops by jumping quickly to one side.

"Ok guys," I said, as they all extended their legs and stood up, "Samantha and I will go first, and then the rest of you as quickly as possible. The gate will only stay open for about ten seconds."

As I gathered my thoughts, I realised that I could feel the Snerks PCM, and sighed in relief. Despite what I had said earlier, I had never been really sure that I could do it. The gate opened, and Samantha and I dived through, moving to one side as quickly as possible to avoid incoming Tolltops. The gate snapped shut.

I had brought us back to Grandpa Kenneth's shed, because I wanted him to hear what Samantha had to say. It would be easy enough to open a door to Tolltopsy to send the guys back with the invasion warning, though whether it would be in time I didn't know. The deciding factor would be the Kriddles and whether they would cooperate in the defence of their reality.

For a few seconds until I sent the Tolltops home, the shed was pretty crowded, even more so when Grandpa, Mum and Dad heard the commotion and crowded in through the door as well.

"No Grandpa," I yelled, and jumped in front of Samantha, as he grabbed a garden fork and was about to stick her. For a second I wondered how it had survived the Snerk raid when everything sharp had been removed, but then I remembered seeing it stuck in the ground outside.

He only just managed not to stick me through the middle, and yelled,

"Get out of the way Robert... She's a Snerk."

"I know Grandpa, but she saved us. If it wasn't for her we would all be roasting by morning. They captured us and she set us free."

Mum laid a hand on Grandpa's arm. He still looked uncertain, but at least he lowered the tines of the fork to the floor. I told them what had happened in Tolltopsy and then Snerkland, finishing with the rescue by Samantha.

"Why can't the Tops just reintroduce the Snerk traps?" asked Dad.

"From what the PCM is telling me now, the Snerks have found out how to shut them down and also how to make the gates any size they want. It's easy, anyone can do it. It's just that nobody thought of it until now. Apparently the gates are flexible and if you grab the edges you can stretch them."

"Ok then," said Mum, "I think it's time for Samantha Snerk here to tell us her story."

"There were four of us," said Samantha as she began her story, "each one was sent out to a different place to find out how easy it would be to invade. My job as you know was here. It didn't take long to understand that, with the weapons you have, we wouldn't stand a chance, and I went back to report this. But I had only just got through the gate when I realised that I had been enjoying myself, and that I liked Kenneth a lot, so I thought I would delay reporting for a while and carry on enjoying myself. It was a strange feeling really. We... Snerks that is... don't have fun, we're much too busy planning nasty things. Eventually, I knew I couldn't delay any longer, so I went back, but it was then that I knew I was in love with Kenneth. Real honest-to-god human love, not like the Snerks have. Impossible of course, so I changed back into a Snerk. The only trouble was that I didn't change… no matter what I did, I stayed in my human form. It was only then that I realised that I couldn't open doors anymore. I had been using ones that Snerks had already opened. So when Attica came and grabbed my clothes and dragged me to the little door he had come through, I managed to stretch it enough to squeeze through myself and follow him to Robert."

Grandpa was staring at her with wide eyes, but then he said, "Robert."

I knew what he wanted, so I picked up the PCM from where it had fallen when I had gone to Tolltopsy, and gave the command, "Turn Samantha back into a Snerk."

Absolutely nothing happened, and a voice whispered into my mind,

"*And neither will it. Real love is rare, and when it appears it should be supported.*"

"Sorry Grandpa," I said, "apparently it's permanent. You might just have to marry the woman."

"Why would I do that Robert?" he asked, but there was just a glint of hope in his eyes.

"Because you were so sad when you admitted that you knew she was a Snerk. Snerk or no Snerk, you are in love with her as a human."

Samantha and Grandpa looked at each, and then she threw herself into his arms. The rest of us just turned our backs in embarrassment. Apart from all the kissing noises, the only thing we heard was the clatter as Grandpa finally dropped the fork onto the floor.

Maybe I was wrong... perhaps she is grandma material after all.

Chapter Eleven

"*Use the shed*," said the voice, and I giggled. Visions of Obi Wan Kenobi out of 'Star Wars' saying 'Use the Force' came into my mind.

"Use it to do what?" I asked, becoming serious.

"*You are wondering how to help the Tops*," it replied.

"Yes but what good is an old shed?"

"*It's only old here. In other places it's different.*"

"Who are you talking to Bobby?" asked Mum.

"The PCM I think," I said, "Its telling me

to use the shed. I'm not quite sure what for, but it does say that the shed is different in other places."

"I've always wondered," said Grandpa, "ever since that night that it suddenly appeared."

That was something that none of us knew, and if looks could fry you, then all of ours turned Grandpa into a crisp,

"Well of course I couldn't tell anyone, you would all have thought I had gone nuts, and probably put me away somewhere. I mean what would you have thought if I had told you that I was in the garden one evening, and a star appeared in front of me, and out of it popped the shed. It frightened the life out of me. Took me days before I could look inside."

"Well what is it when it goes to other places?" I asked him.

"No idea," said Grandpa, "you'll have to take it and find out."

"Ok then, everyone out, and I'll give it a bash."

"*No you'll need a crew.*"

"**Stop**," I shouted at their departing backs, "I've been told I'll need a crew.

"How many?" I asked silently.

"*Oh,three should do nicely. It wouldn't be right to take Samantha.*"

I realised what the PCM really meant, and I stopped Samantha as she was coming back in.

"Not you Samantha. We'd love to have you along, but if all goes to plan it wouldn't be right for you to be involved."

"No Snerk has ever been worried about the death of another one," she said, "and wherever your grandpa goes then so do I. Besides which, I am human now... completely."

The look on her face and the sound in her voice was enough. I stepped aside and she came in.

"I'd better lock the door from the inside," said Dad, and held out his hand for the PCM. I passed it to him, and he pushed it into the lock and closed the door. As soon as it closed, he pulled the key out and the lock made a clacking sound as it locked. The sun was just coming up and there was no point in hanging about. From my experience of the Snerks I knew they'd move earlier than intended when they discovered we had escaped so, "Take us and the shed to Tolltopsy," I said.

The inside of the shed changed before my eyes, it shot out in all directions until it was at least ten times its original size, becoming sleek and streamlined. There were instruments everywhere, and all of us found ourselves seated in front of them, wearing some quite nice blue uniforms. I was positioned at what was obviously the flight controls though I had no idea how I knew what they were. Everyone else seemed to know what they were doing as well, so I just concentrated on what was in front of me. It was all familiar, as if I had done it a thousand times. Through the forward ports I saw the edges of a gate pass us and the landscape of Tolltopsy come into view. Everything felt so much smaller, until I realised that it was actually me that was larger. I seemed to have become an adult without actually growing up.

Everything about the craft was already in my mind, as if it had always been there, including the fact that I was in Command. Our flight was a bit erratic at that moment, so I reached out to the controls without thinking and made some slight adjustments to steady us down. Our speed was considerable, and with our nose pointed skyward we shot upwards.

"Tactical... Starboard weapons report please," I heard myself ask.

"Particle beam cannon online sir," said Dad, "Lasers are just powering up and fléchettes are ready to deploy."

"Port?"

"Ditto Starboard Sir," added Mum.

Grandpa's Shed

I had never heard of the word fléchette before, but I knew what it meant. It referred to our arsenal of tiny steel slivers that were fired in bursts at very high speed. They would certainly penetrate the Snerks armour. It was the perfect weapon. I brought the craft around in a wide sweep, and headed downwards. Oddly, I didn't feel afraid. Perhaps it was my parents calling me 'Sir' that made the difference.

Below I could see that a massive gate was open. It seemed to be getting larger all the time as two odd looking devices attached to each edge slowly drew apart. Snerks in their thousands were pouring through. Hundreds upon hundreds of Kriddles were diving down and taking at least two Snerks each in their two mouths. But it was not working as I had hoped. The armour might not stop my fléchettes, but it was definitely preventing the Kriddles from biting into them. The Kriddles were being cut to pieces by the swords, and apart from fleeing as they were now doing there was little they could do to protect themselves. The Tolltops were nowhere to be seen, already having fled. Who could blame them? Against this army they were helpless. It seems that the Tops who I had returned to Tolltopsy had managed to warn them in time.

This was the ideal moment to act, while they were still massed inside the gate. If I waited much longer they would be too dispersed for our single ship to be effective. A hail of fléchettes, travelling at supersonic speeds into those massed ranks, would hopefully decimate them enough to make them stop and think. It looked like the only hope we had and an opportunity not to be missed.

"Wait until the last Kriddle is clear," I said, "then we'll do a run and let them taste the fléchettes."

"I'll unload the lot in a wide sweep," said Dad, "with a bit of luck it will scare the rest to death."

"I'll coordinate with starboard sir," said Mum,

Keeping my course to run across the face of the open gate, I lined up the nose and opened her up. We rocketed in, and I watched in fascination as the fléchettes left the front of the craft like a spreading mist, albeit a very rapidly moving one. I saw the leading edge of the mist touch the massed ranks of Snerks, who dissolved into raging clouds of purple smoke, leaving behind a one hundred metre wide swathe full of dissolving Snerk skins.

It was over almost before it had started. I know it didn't bother Snerks all that much when one of their own got killed, but the amount, and the ease with which we did it must have put the fear of God into them. As one, the entire army, or what was left of it, streamed back through the gate, helped on their way by some well place fire from the aft particle cannons manned by Grandpa and Samantha. The gate snapped shut as soon as the last one had passed through.

Almost immediately hoards of Kriddles appeared, zooming downwards and through the purple smoke, taking great mouthfuls on their way, until only small wisps remained. Then as one, they dipped a pair of wings to me and started to make altitude, finally disappearing away to the west.

I briefly circled the carnage to check for any stragglers, but our first run had been more effective than even I had hoped and nothing apart from a horrendous amount of dissolving Snerk skins was left. I brought the craft down towards a relatively clean spot and settled it carefully onto the ground, mainly because I wanted to have a look and see what it looked like from the outside. Everyone else seemed to have the same idea, as there was a mad scramble for the airlock almost as soon as the sound of the engines died. Silly really as we all already knew anyway.

We came out of the craft to be besieged by thousands of Tolltops, who seemed to be emerging from the ground itself, screaming and shouting with joy. It was definitely a celebration to end all celebrations, with non-stop dancing and singing everywhere we looked. We didn't get away until well into the night, but finally we boarded the craft and headed back into the real world.

"How did the shed get to Tolltopsy Grandpa," asked Little Bridget, looking up at me with her giant and quite startling green eyes.

"I never really saw it for myself," I said, "but Attica was watching and he said the Shed just seemed to collapse into a star and disappear."

"But what did the shed look like then Grandpa," asked little Robert, who was sitting next to little Bridget in the semi-circle of seven eager young faces in front of me.

I smiled. I always thought of my grandchildren as little and try as I might I could never visualise their names without adding 'little' at the front. Whenever they visited, they always asked for the same story. Their parents knew it by heart, as it had been something that they had been brought up with, but they refused to tell their own kids, saying that no-one told it like me.

It always started the same way, with one or the other asking,

"Why do you keep that grotty old shed Grandpa Robert?"

And then I would reply,

"Well there's a story attached to that, would you like to hear it?"

Their parents told me it was the only time they got any peace, and I was convinced that they put the kids up to it.

"Grandpa, what did it look like," insisted little Robert, bringing me back to the present.

From where I sat, I could see the shed in the garden through the kitchen window, and I smiled quietly to myself as two small round figures, hand in hand disappeared through the open door. It was always nice when *Almost* Frettle's own grandchildren visited. Well not really *Almost*. He had been *Complete* for a good many years now.

I reached down and lifted Robert up on to my knee, and looking down into his wide blue, and intensely inquisitive eyes, I said,

"Well almost exactly like Grandpa's Shed Robert."

From the back I could see that little Katy

was trying to get up the courage to ask a question. She was the gentlest of them all, and would break into floods of tears if someone swatted a fly or stood on a spider. I had a good idea what she wanted to know. It had never been asked before, and I had always steered the conversation away. But it had to be faced sometime, so gently I said, "What would you like to know Katy?

For a second it seemed that she wouldn't say anything, but then she suddenly blurted, "What happened to Attica Grandpa?"

"He had a pretty good life," I said sadly, because even to this day I missed him, "and lived quite a bit longer than most cats. I was in my early thirties when he died. He was twenty-six."

I felt a tear form and then roll down my face. But it was OK. The kids got up and crowded around me to 'hug Grandpa better'

"I'm so sorry Grandpa," whispered little Katy, with her arms around my neck.

For me it was a lovely end, to what I always saw as a lovely story. Now though, as a single word whispered into my mind, I knew that the time had finally arrived for me to hand over the responsibility that I had held for so many years. It had been more of a pleasure than I can say, but eventually all good things must come to an end.

"Katy," I said, holding out the PCM, "I think this belongs to you now."

The End

Why not write a review?

This book is independently published, and as authors we rise or fall on our reviews, and any publicity that we can get. So if you can write a review, now that you have read the book, I would appreciate it. The only thing I ask is that the review be an honest reflection of your opinion. I am not too concerned as to whether that opinion is good or bad, all I ask is that you actually give one. You can post your reviews on Amazon, or where acceptable with other retailers.

Finally, if you enjoy this, or any of my other books, then please spread the word.

My best regards to you all.

Robert A.V, Jacobs

ravjacobs@hotmail.com

Character list

Robert – The hero of our story.

Grandpa Robert - Robert all grown up.

Grandpa Kenneth - Robert's Grandpa

Mum - Robert's mum.

Dad - Robert's dad.

Samantha - The love of Grandpa Kenneth's life and an ex-Snerk.

James - Robert's friend.

Snerks - Race of vicious triangular beings from an alternate reality.

Tolltops - A race of round ball shaped beings from a second alternate reality.

Gridlins - A race of sort of round flat sieve like beings from a third alternate reality.

Tenpids - A race of tubular beings with ten legs from a fourth alternate reality.

Little Robert, Little Bridget, Little Katy - Three of Grandpa Robert's grandchildren.

Binlod - Snerk masquerading as a Tolltop.

Almost **Frettle** - A child Tolltop and Robert's friend.

Virtually **Wendum** - *Almost* Frettle's mum.

Complete **Lodtron** - *Almost* Frettle's dad.

PCM - Principle Conundrum Manipulator.

Other books by the Author

Because this book is predominantly for younger readers, allow me to share excerpts from some of my other books in this genre.

The first will be from my latest book which is about Witches, and is entitled 'Cindy Lost and the Black Witch'

So if you have enjoyed this book, I urge you to give Cindy a try.

A short Excerpt from:

**Cindy Lost
and the Black Witch**

Chapter One

The first time Cindy Lost realised that there was something not quite right about her, was the day that she set the cat's tail on fire. It took quite a while to catch him and put it out, and by the time she had done that, there was very little of the tail left.

The cat was only being playful, but he had jumped on her favourite doll, and torn its dress with his claws. She had yelled at him, and waved a stick that she had found in the garden.

She couldn't remember what she had said, but there was a big whoosh and the tail was in flames.

The cat was running around in circles shrieking, and she grabbed her doll's blanket, and eventually managed to get close enough to throw it over him and douse the flames.

As soon as she had him extinguished, she yelled for her mother who, as it happens, had already heard the cat and was on her way.

"I've warned you about playing with matches," she said crossly, flicking her long blond hair from her face, "we have to get him to the Vet. I'll deal with you later."

"But mum," she protested, as her mother lifted the cat into her arms, "I wasn't playing with matches. I just waved that stick at him."

"**What!**" exclaimed her mother, dropping the cat, whose day it obviously was not, onto the ground, "Where did you get that?"

"I just found it in the garden."

"That was your father's. He always said that it was a souvenir of Hogsthorpe. I *knew* that there was something strange about him."

"What was strange mum?"

"Never mind I'll explain later. Right now we have to fix the cat. Wave the stick at him and say something."

"But I don't know any Latin mum, and if

you expect me to be a Witch, and do Witch things, they always say things in Latin."

"Don't believe things that you see in films, or read in books. You set his tail on fire and you didn't know any Latin then either."

"That's true." said Cindy, and picking up the stick, she visualised a magnificent hairy tail, and added loudly, "Make the cat's tail better."

The recoil and the massive flash from the stick, deposited her several yards away on her backside, the cat gave an uncharacteristic yowl, and then ran away down the garden, bushy tail trailing behind.

"Well," said her mother, with some satisfaction, "that appears to have fixed that."

Cindy got to her feet, stretched herself up to an impressive one metre, sixty two and a half centimetres, which all of her friends said was pretty tall for a twelve year old, and said sternly, "I believe you now have something to tell me mother."

"Let's go indoors. We don't really need neighbours listening in to *this* conversation."

Safely in the house, and settled in a couple of easy chairs, Cindy was the first to speak.

"You said a souvenir of Hogsthorpe mum," she said, "you were kidding right. I bet there's no such place."

"Actually, there is. I didn't believe it either until your father showed it to me on the map. It's just a few miles south of Mablethorpe on the east coast of England. But never mind that. I had hoped that there wouldn't be any need for explanations, but it seems that you have inherited more from your father than I had hoped."

She paused.

"I met your father about twelve years ago. Even that was quite odd. I couldn't understand how he could have appeared when a minute ago there was no one there. But my, was he gorgeous. I wasn't even concerned about how he had managed to get into my lounge without coming through the front door. Right at that minute I decided that I was going to marry him even if I had to kidnap him. He must have felt the same way, because for a minute he was speechless."

Her mind drifted back to that evening twelve years ago.

"I'm lost," he had replied, but then hesitantly added as if he'd never had a last name, "A-A-Alec Lost... Who are you? You seem vaguely familiar."

"I didn't believe that his name was 'Lost'," she explained to Cindy, "but he did seem very confused, so I thought I would go along with it, besides which right than I fancied him something rotten. And who really cares about names anyway."

"My name is Jean fellows," I told him, "and I'm pretty sure that we've never met before... though I wish that we had."

"We were inseparable from that moment on," she concluded, "and were married four weeks later."

"But how does that tell me why I can suddenly do magic?"

"Because I think he was a Witch, or at least he could do magic, and so can you, judging from one unfortunate cat's tail. You seem to have inherited that from him, certainly not from me, because I couldn't magic spit if my life depended on it. He never confided in me, but I'm not daft and there were too many strange things in our marriage to ignore. For instance I asked him to make a cup of tea once, and it came far too quickly to be natural. So I made an excuse and went into the kitchen. The kettle was cold. I have to admit, though, that when I pointed it out to him, he seemed genuinely puzzled. I suspect that he never knew that he was doing it."

"Which, I suspect, is why you didn't act like a normal mum, and run away screaming when you saw what I had done?"

"Pretty much," her mother said, "Once, I saw him reach for the wand, or stick as you call it, and I swear that it lifted up to meet his hand. I did wonder where it had gone, because it disappeared when he died."

Cindy had dropped the stick onto the floor when she had sat down, and on impulse experimentally reached for it. Even though she half expected it, she was still surprised when it actually did rise up to meet her hand. Right at that moment she was almost overwhelmed by the knowledge that she could do pretty much anything she liked. Perhaps it was fortunate that she had the mother that she did.

"Don't even think about it," her mother said, "that wand gets locked away until we can find someone who can teach you how to use it properly."

"Perhaps I can be of assistance,"

It was a voice from behind her chair, and their mouths dropped open when a real pointy hat and pointy eared Goblin walked out.

"My name is Ear Wax," he announced, "I was supposed to be here a couple of years ago, when you reached ten. Witches usually display some indication of their powers when they reach that age, but for some reason you didn't, so the council effectively wrote you off. But the cat's tail really threw the cat amongst the pigeons, so to speak, and as a result, you have suddenly become quite famous."

"And what exactly are you?" demanded Jean, reaching for a poker from the fireplace, "What are you talking about, and where did you come from?"

"Me? Oh I'm only a Goblin, and there is no need for violence." said Ear Wax, holding his arms up to protect himself, "I came from your glass cabinet to tell you that your daughter is a Witch."

Cindy grinned. Life was starting to become extremely interesting.

"And what sort of a name is 'Ear Wax'?" she asked, deciding to ignore the glass cabinet.

"I might ask the same about Cindy Lost," he said indignantly, "at least it's not 'Stomach Acid' like my cousin."

"Ok then, if what you say is true," said Jean, placing the poker back in the fireplace, and suspecting that she would not like the answer, "how will you be able to help?"

"We used to have a school for Witches, but it had to close when the number of Witches suddenly declined about a couple of hundred years ago, probably because people started burning them. Instead they formed the Witches Tutoring Guild, to cover the few that appeared from time to time."

"So you are my teacher then?" asked Cindy.

"Only one of them," said the Goblin, "I am one of six, and I am your pyrotechnic advisor."

"Stopping or starting?" asked Cindy, grinning, "and bear in mind that I have had some practice."

"We must start as we mean to continue," he said, straight faced, "perhaps a period as a worm might make you more respectful?"

Cindy gulped, "I'm sorry sir," she said hastily, in no doubt at all that he was quite capable of carrying out his threat.

"I like you Ear Wax," declared Jean, grinning broadly, and showing a lot more confidence than she was actually feeling, "a period as a worm... I love it."

"One thing does puzzle us in the guild though," he said addressing Jean, "and that's the business with the wand. Wands usually die with their owner, and we can't figure out why this one didn't. Wands always choose their first and only owner shortly after being made, and we've never heard of one transferring its power to someone else."

End of Excerpt

Other books by the Author

The second book that I intend to spotlight here is the first in a series about Daisy Weal, a half human, half alien little girl with superpowers. This book is entitled 'Daisy Weal' and introduces Daisy at the moment of her birth, until she reaches ten years old.

So if you have enjoyed this book, and the excerpt of Cindy's, I urge you to give Daisy Weal a try.

A Short Excerpt from:

Daisy Weal

Chapter One

Definitely the most odd of places.

It started as a fairly unassuming day at 12 Trendal Place, Bishops Ashton. The sun was trying hard to break through a grey misty sky, with limited success. It had been raining on and off for a number of days, and everything was damp and glistening, in the hazy sunshine. A slight breeze ruffled the, still wet, lush green lawns, which had grown at least six inches since they had last received attention.

Everything had taken on a dark and leaden feeling, and the silence hung hard in the street and surrounding areas, waiting with bated breath it seemed, for the inevitable sounds of lawn mowers and strimmers, to intrude into this all too brief period of tranquillity.

In the distance towards the town centre, the sounds of life were more normal, with the noise of traffic and the occasional horn 'beep' from an impatient motorist, wafting in on the slight movement of air. A large aircraft passed overhead, out of sight in the sky above the grey, its engines in full voice as it gained height from the nearby international airport. *Probably off to some exotic place*, thought Marjorie Weal, as she stood in her doorway to take a deep breath of the cool and damp morning air. Against the cold, she had pulled on a coat over her night dress, but had kept on her slippers rightly considering, that being large fluffy and pink; they would be warmer than shoes. She leaned against the door frame, waiting for the milkman and wishing that her pregnancy was over. *Nine months is too long.* she thought and then giggled to herself, *Women should have been designed with three months in mind.*

A milk float whined to a stop at the head of the street, and the clink of bottles broke the silence as the milkman began his deliveries. He muttered, "Pig of a mornin' init," as he stood aside at the gate of number ten to let the postman pass, and then followed him up the path to the front door.

"Yeh, but the sun keeps trying," was returned.

Marjorie walked slowly down the few metres to her front gate to wait for the postman as he came out of next door, and was greeted with:

"Mornin' Ms Weal, nothing today I'm afraid; would only have been bills anyway; Baby due soon? Have you thought of a name yet?"

"Very soon thank-you, but not today I hope," observed Marjorie, "Well if it's a girl we're calling her Daisy, haven't made up our mind if it's a boy."

"Well you take yourself inside. It's no day for you to be out and about in your condition. Don't you agree Joe?" the postman nodded to the Milkman as he approached.

Joe handed two bottles of half fat pasteurised milk to Marjorie, and said,

"You do as the man says Ms Weal. He should know he's got six kids."

Marjorie nodded, and then turned and walked toward her front door. She had only walked a couple of paces when the first contraction hit, "Oh, George," she gasped, as she doubled over. The pains became intense and rapid and she dropped to her knees, the two bottles of milk fell from her hands, and rolled down the path as she grabbed her stomach.

"You see to her, I'll get Mr Weal," said Joe, ignoring the rolling bottles as he vaulted over Marjorie, and rushed to the front door,

"Mr Weal, Mr Weal," he shouted, through the open door.

It all became a blur for Marjorie after that. All she knew was that the pains were too close. There had been no build up, and it was all too sudden. Then George was kneeling beside her and taking her hand.

"Hang on, the ambulance is on its way; you'll be OK," and then, "I hope!" she heard him mutter under his breath.

Then the ambulance arrived, and it seemed that they were at the hospital almost instantly. Before she knew it, she was being manhandled onto a stretcher, lights were rushing past, a nurse appeared, and the pain stopped.

Through bleary eyes she saw the doctor approaching with a bundle in his hands,

"It's a girl," he grinned and turned the bundle to face Marjorie. All she could see was an enormous set of green eyes looking at her from this wonderful little face. The eyes turned and looked straight toward her.

"Well I'm glad that's over," said Daisy.

The nurse folded in on herself and crumpled to the ground. The doctor threw Daisy straight up into the air, as he fainted and fell over backwards, knocking trolleys and instruments in all directions. Marjorie being made of sterner stuff just went to sleep again. Somehow, Daisy had landed in the crib, the right way around and perfectly centred. She gurgled happily to herself because after all, she was a baby. *This is definitely the most odd of places*, she thought. Then the door flew open, and more people rushed in.

"What has happened here?" demanded a very stern looking nurse.

"Oh they all fainted," said Daisy.

Three more people joined the heap on the floor. But the stern looking nurse, who had not been looking at Daisy, swivelled around with eyes that were deep, dark, and accusing. That gaze was obviously designed to reduce lesser nurses to jelly, and from the fear on the faces of the others, it was very effective indeed.

"Who said that?" she bellowed.

"Now, now," muttered Marjorie, who had still not quite woken up, but had been disturbed by the racket, "not so much noise, you'll frighten the baby. I suggest that you get some help to remove all these fainted bodies. I do declare that people will fall over at the drop of a hat these days."

The nurse took one more look around, swivelled about and swept from the room.

"Hello Mum," said Daisy.

Marjorie being full of gas and air, which apparently is given to aid difficult births, was so convinced that she was hallucinating, that she thought she would play along with her imagination for a little while, or at least, until the effects wore off. So, dreamily she said,

"This really is something that I have to get my head around, but in the meantime dear, please remember that you are a baby, and until we are alone, you only know how to gurgle. Babies don't speak for at least a couple of years."

"How odd," said Daisy "can I talk to Dad?"

"Not a good idea. Having a baby is hard enough on the poor dear, but one that talks might be too much. I think it would be better if we kept this as our little secret for the time being. Now shush, someone is coming," replied Marjorie, realising at last, that this was indeed real, and that she was neither hallucinating nor dreaming.

The bodies were removed, revived, and sent somewhere to 'rest until they were feeling better'. A pair of security guards walked up and stationed themselves at her door, and then people in suits started to appear. They were milling around, talking heatedly, and pausing periodically to look towards Marjorie. Then one important looking man, removed himself from the mêlée, and strode purposefully towards her door.

"I understand that your baby spoke… " he started to say.

"Do you?" interrupted Marjorie, who by now, had virtually recovered from her medications. She knew that to prevent unwanted intrusion into her life and that of her new baby, she would have to quickly take control of the situation.

"Then you are a bigger fool than you look. Here she is, no more than an hour old," she continued, trying desperately not to laugh, and at the same time sound sarcastic,

"Go on, look; she won't bite. Does she look as if she can speak? Or is the word of a group of people, who have trouble remaining conscious, of paramount importance here?"

"I have… " he tried again.

"No you don't," said Marjorie, interrupting him again. "What you have to do is to look at my baby, then remove yourself and the guards, and let us get some rest. Oh, and find my husband, he must be worried sick."

The man looked confused and about to say something else, but instead he bent over the crib, and said, "Hello," to Daisy.

Daisy stared up at him, smiled happily, dribbled a little, and said, "goo."

The rest of the stay in the hospital was fairly uneventful, with the normal comings and goings, of a busy maternity unit. The members of staff, who had attended her in the beginning and then had been carried out, didn't appear in the department again. So, for a little while, no-one had time for any pleasantries until replacements were found. There were still whispers and quick glances towards her, but no-one bothered her.

George, came in as often as his work would allow, and then sat holding Marjorie's hand, staring at the baby for hours on end. Sometimes, he arrived so tired that he fell asleep with his head cradled in Marjorie's arms.

"He is so tired," whispered Daisy.

"He's a good man Daisy," said Marjorie, "who wants to make a good life for us. He works too hard, so I think we can let him sleep for a while."

Those enormous green eyes stared

silently at Marjorie for a few seconds.

"You were expecting me before you married him, weren't you?" asked Daisy.

There was no accusation in the voice, or in the eyes. It was just a question that Marjorie wished hadn't been asked, but now that it had, it could not be avoided.

"One morning I woke up pregnant. No idea how or when or even what happened. I can't remember any of it. I hadn't even been out drinking," then she added, "Might have been better if I had, but it was done, so no point worrying. I had to accept it. I suppose, the only good thing was that I had no relatives to judge me. Well, apart from my sister Harriet of course. She just stuck her nose in the air, and disowned me. Not a great loss, as she was never a particularly nice person. Anyway, a month later, I met George. We hit it off right away, and were married within a couple of weeks. I have never regretted it," she finished firmly.

"Who are you talking to love?" asked George sleepily.

"Just myself, George, just myself," she soothed, "You had better go home, and get some sleep. I did mean to ask before you go. Did you remember to call your mum in Hawaii, with the news?"

Millicent Daisy Weal was George's

mother. She had moved to Hawaii with her American second husband shortly after meeting him while on holiday there. She had been worried about George's reaction to the news, but he had been full of enthusiasm and encouragement. So, she had departed, totally in love, for a little house just outside of Waikiki. Her happiness, unfortunately, was short lived, as her new husband died only three years after their marriage. But she loved Hawaii, and chose to stay. Without fail however, she phoned George and Marjorie once a week, and sometimes twice a week since Marjorie's pregnancy.

"Oh god no, she will kill me," he replied, "I'd better get home, and do that. I'll see you tomorrow." He bent over, kissed her, then Daisy, gave a quick wave, and was gone.

For the next few days that Marjorie was required to stay in the hospital, George always came and spent a couple of hours with them, never missing an opportunity to pick up Daisy and drool over her. Marjorie was never sure whether Daisy appreciated all the cooings and 'who's Daddie's liddle girl then', but she played along just fine, with large amounts of dribble and gurgling to keep him happy.

Finally the day came when all the medical specialists, though still suspicious, could find no further excuse to keep them in the hospital, and reluctantly agreed to allow them to go home the next day. George was visibly delighted.

He arrived bright and early the following day, happily wheeling a brightly decorated chair which was laden down with very bright pink baby clothes, pink toys, and perched on top, was a pink carry cot.

Oh God, thought Marjorie, who quietly hated pink, and Daisy just giggled.

End of Excerpt

About the Author

Born in the Royal Military Hospital in Portsmouth, England in 1938, he attended Titchfield (Hampshire, UK) Primary School and Fareham (Hampshire, UK) Secondary Modern Boys School until 1953.

He joined the Royal Air Force as an Apprentice in 1955 and served 14 years, being discharged in 1968. During that period, in 1962, he met and married Kim, and they are still together 55 years later. After a short period as a Prison Officer, he entered the Computer Industry with Golden Wonder Ltd and stayed in that profession with various companies until 1991. He then joined an Inner City Medical Practice in Leicester (Leicestershire UK) as Fundholding Manager and Practice Manager until his retirement in 2003. After spending thirteen years dividing his time between his home in Leicester and Sax, a small town near Alicante in Spain, he has now moved permanently back to the UK and lives in Oadby, Leicestershire.

For more information about Robert and his books, please visit his website at:
http://ravjacobs.wixsite.com/robertavjacobs